PRAISE FOR
TOXIC SHOCK AND OTHER FAMILY GATHERINGS

The linked stories in Jude Klassen's Toxic Shock and Other Family Gatherings are never less than incisive, bittersweet, funny and, best of all, feel true to life. Family foibles and fathers and sisters in particular, are the gist of it. There isn't a single story that doesn't ring with relatable comedy and subdued anger at the intricacies of putting up with parents, siblings and relatives. As Klassen's central character Kerry discovers, some men are the same at 70 as they were at 17; entitled, opinionated and dull. Sisters are steady friends until they're not. Mothers never seem to change. Christmas gatherings are epic, fraught and, maybe in memory, dark comedy.

There are searing vignettes here, of childhood, adolescent life and female adulthood attached to people you'd avoid if you weren't related. At times this brilliant book is a tragicomic family saga and at times it's beautifully funny-poignant, but never less than penetrating and entertaining.

— John Doyle, bestselling author and former Globe and Mail columnist.

In *Toxic Shock and Other Family Gatherings*, Jude Klassen introduces us to the unforgettable Kerry as she navigates small town British Columbia in the 70s and 80s, Vancouver and Edmonton in the 90s, and Toronto in the 2000s. Beautifully observed, Klassen's stunning prose lands us in the middle of Kerry's most vulnerable, transformative moments with wit, humour, and lyricism. Sharp, succinct, wise, tender, and profound.

— Carmen Aguirre, int. bestselling author of *Something Fierce: Memoirs of a Revolutionary Daughter*.

Ms. Klassen's stories of multiple generations, some living hardscrabble lives holding tenuous secrets, are compelling for their imagery and stark revelatory humour. Truth can be "simple and painless" she writes, then proves it is anything but. The ordinary becomes extraordinary in this ambitious collection where "even death has a happy ending, full of white light."

There is knowledge and insight on these pages.

— **David Sherman author of *Momma's Got the Blues* and Playwright, *The Daily Miracle*.**

Jude Klassen writes with trenchant humour and pained-love about family tensions, generational discord, coming of age angst, consummate trashy behavior and neanderthal-like opinions on climate change with a thought-filled-light-hearted spirit that leaves us cheering for anyone threatening to help zoo animals escape on a full moon.

— **Ewan Whyte author of *Shifting Paradigms: Essays on Art and Culture*.**

Jude Klassen has the uncanny ability to make you laugh and feel desperate at the same time. Her raw talent to tap into the insanity and love within all families is there on every single page.

— **Kathleen Goldhar award-winning producer/host *Do you Know Mordechai?* CBC's *Crime Story*.**

Reading Jude Klassen's literary debut, I am pleased, but not surprised. The heartfelt, gritty ingenuity of her films easily transmits to the printed page. Stories of femmes and freaks coalesce into a colourful, charismatic collection.

—**C.E. Hoffman, author of *Losers and Freaks***

TOXIC SHOCK
AND OTHER FAMILY GATHERINGS

STORIES
JUDE KLASSEN

Title: Toxic Shock and Other Family Gatherings
Names: Klassen, Jude, author.
Description: Short Stories
Identifiers:
(print) ISBN: 978-1-0688407-0-8
(e-book) ISBN: 978-1-0688407-1-5
(Audio) ISBN: 978-1-0688407-2-2

Judecast Productions Inc. respectfully acknowledges that the land on which we operate is the Traditional Territory of many Nations, including the Anishinabeg, the Wendat, and the Haudenosaunee. It is also the Treaty Lands of the Mississaugas of the Credit.

Jude Klassen gratefully acknowledges the Canada Council for the Arts for their financial support in the form of an Explorations Literary Grant to complete this collection.

For my gift of beauty, Mikhael Klassen-Kay, who wasn't even born when my first story in this collection was published and is now my trusted editor.

And for my beloved parents who gave me the freedom to write by not reading my work—even when they were alive.

"Drugs and alcohol will get you through the holiday season."

Kerry Wiebe on Christmas
with the family.

TABLE OF CONTENTS

WESTERN ALIENATION

Toronto, 2007

Through the screened kitchen window, Kerry looks down at her parents drinking cocktails with her husband on the shady back deck of her Toronto cottage. Her mother, Dollie, sips her G&T and absently buffs the tabletop with her serviette. Kerry's father, Matt, a retired surgeon, nurses a Scotch. Simply by his posture—shoulders thrown back, legs apart—Kerry can tell he has a buzz on and is happily winding up for one of his King of the World rants.

After decades of scrolling through a multitude of overtly left-wing boys, Kerry has pleased her father (and relieved her mother) by settling down and actually marrying a man. Strapping, dark, and confident, Andrew looks good uncorking wine and manning the barbecue. And although he doesn't watch sports, go grouse hunting, or open beer bottles with his teeth, his amusing stories of uncles harvesting squirrels for pies and raising trout in swimming pools have earned him entry into the club.

Before she returns to the back deck, Kerry cranks the Frank Sinatra CD playing on the kitchen stereo. Maybe her dad will be distracted and burst into song, forgetting to continue verbally disembowelling David Suzuki. Just maybe, Old Blue Eyes will also save her from having to defend all the usual suspects: the environment, same-sex marriage, the separation of church and state. It's all become a little draining. Her parents are old. She knows she should probably just shut up and let the esteemed doctor light his tire fires and go harshly into that good night.

Although it is still early June, a heat wave hit them the day her parents arrived from Abbotsford, rumpled from the red eye. They are on day four of their seven-day visit, and each morning has begun with gorgeous late spring light and a smog warning. Kerry slides back into her chair in time to hear Andrew apologize for the air quality.

Her dad sips his Scotch and grimaces. "I guess it's all that global warming."

"Of course," says Kerry, her fingers stiff around the stem of her wineglass.

He grunts. "Wasn't serious."

"I was."

These short bursts have replaced the passionate arguments. Instead of attacking, Kerry smiles and imagines a single-panel comic strip. In it, a cartoon version of her dad stands surrounded by rushing water. Fires blaze behind him, a tornado sweeps in from the left. His grandchild dangles limply in his arms, a gas mask strapped to her ashen face. The caption reads, "There's no such thing as global goddamn warming."

Kerry's pretty sure that given the chance, her dad would have been one of those cocksure corporate spokesmen in the fifties who cheerfully swilled nuclear waste to prove it was safe. Safety: her mother has Catholicism, her father has the Fraser Institute, and although it is cowardly, Kerry cools her own heated head by reminding herself that nothing will matter to her in fifty-odd years. Of course, placating herself this way worked better before she procreated. Now she has a child, perfect pale Katerina, the unexpected gift of beauty.

Kerry imagines decades from now, describing her own youth to her incredulous daughter. *You could swim right in the lake. You could leave the house without carrying a canister of oxygen.*

Even when you were small, we had real birds flapping around our backyard. We had a birdbath—remember? There was a cardinal that attacked his own reflection in our window—you screamed with laughter. Already her stories of four-wheeling with illiterate boys, buying acid from strangers in downtown Vancouver, and slathering herself in baby oil while sprawled in the midday sun seem psychotic to Kerry. And they certainly lack charm when contrasted with her grandmother making her own hats and sausage, or her mother "fighting the good war" by drawing stocking seams down the backs of her legs and jitterbugging with men in uniform.

Kerry watches a maple key spiral into her dad's heavy tumbler of Scotch. She inherited a whole set of the impressive glassware from her mom's only brother, Uncle Piotr, and it strikes her that perhaps Uncle P. is taking aim at his old opponent's drink from wherever decent, angry people go after they die.

Matt glares at the mammoth maple tree shading the small glass table. "Messy bastard." He plucks out the maple key and snaps it over the edge of the deck like a beer cap.

Kerry looks around. The deck has an unkempt sticky look she didn't notice before her parents arrived. A pink plastic dollhouse flags the otherwise invisible drop-off between the two levels of deck. The dollhouse is filthy; Kerry refuses to scrub its many fussy little rooms, particularly the yellow faux-tile bathroom, as grim as any toilet in an auto body shop.

Kat doesn't notice the squalor. She'll happily move her grinning blonde doll family from room to room, shove the husband into the bathtub with his apron-clad wife, upend the baby in the grimy sink, or wash the cocker spaniel by repeatedly ramming his plastic head into the toilet bowl. And so what? She can build up her immunity, and it's not as though she risks being stabbed with a dirty needle.

"Yeah, we like it in The Beaches, the big trees cut at least some of the pollution." Kerry cringes. *Wrong word.*

Matt blows air through his lips. "Those old growth forests don't provide as much oxygen as new growth. New trees create oxygen as they grow." He tosses back his remaining Scotch and crash-lands the tumbler on the glass table.

Kerry snaps. "Who imparted that bit of wisdom, Frum and Frummer?"

Andrew interjects. "Even if that were true, there are species that depend on old growth habitat for their survival."

Matt snorts. "I'd wipe my arse with a spotted owl."

"Nice." Kerry doesn't bother looking at Andrew. She knows this line will be added to her dad's greatest quotes list. It's the kind of line that used to crack her up, the kind she waited for. Now it just flattens her. Depressing, like the smog and the dirty dollhouse: her father, Kat's Grandpa, wiping his ass with a spotted owl.

The next morning hits hot and grey, as wholesome as breakfast at Wal-Mart. Andrew slumps past, eyeshades pushed up against his dark hair like an absurd headband. He looks out the window and smiles tightly. He doesn't need to explain why they have to live here. No need to remind Kerry that Vancouver is a beautiful tight-fisted bitch who charges five hundred bucks just to let you crash on her futon, while Toronto, the dowager aunt, might chain smoke while you eat, but at least she gives you a job.

Kerry is past caring. She only wishes she had some kind of special suit, the sort of thing an astronaut might wear. Something lightweight and protective she could easily slip on herself and her daughter, so they could comfortably play on the moon.

Because of Katerina, Kerry is actually awake before her father. She has always been an excellent sleeper—in fact, her ability to sleep like a champion kept her looking deceptively fresh. But since giving birth, she is dumbfounded to discover stiff strands of grey hair, a furrow of concern in her forehead, and a small roll of lethargic flesh slumped above her low-waist jeans that no amount of yoga can eradicate. Apparently, there is even a name for this: a pooch. Hideous. Some old prick came up with that one, some old prick with hair on his ass and a twenty-year-old on his arm.

"What?" Andrew pauses at the bathroom door.

"I didn't say anything."

"You look upset."

Kerry knows he really wants to say *you look angry*. She can feel the buzzing in her jaw she gets from clamping down on all that empty space. "Just tired." Christ, that's attractive. She tries again, "Just need an espresso. I feel kinda stunned."

A flash of sadness passes over Andrew's face as he ducks into the bathroom. What does he see? His wife, this burnt-out brunette, standing at the sink. The same woman he once brainstormed with late into the night, the same woman he tipped back a dozen Malpeque oysters with as they swilled cava at sunset. The same woman he used to fuck on the staircase because they couldn't wait to make it three more yards to the bedroom. Kerry stares at the closed bathroom door: the faded paint, the fingerprints, and across the bottom, a streak of what might be spaghetti sauce or red crayon. She stares until the door is a soft white blur and the red slash a knife wound.

Matt thumps up the stairs from the basement guest room, singing. His voice is deep and resonant, and the hymn is something Mennonite, heavy, triumphant. The singing cuts through it all: the morning smog, her lumpen thoughts, the slippery crust that seems to be on everything from her eyes to the ancient appliances. Kerry knows that someday not far in the future, she will be unable to withstand certain music, her father's music: Charlie Rich, Tommy Hunter, Mahalia Jackson. Even the *What's New Pussycat* man, Tom Jones, will knock her to her knees—and not because she's tearing off her panties.

The past and the future have become warring factions, and Kerry must arm herself against their propaganda. Small skirmishes break out constantly, the past lobbing images, sounds, smells: her mother's perfume, the Sunday roast, her father and her uncles harmonizing to *How Great Thou Art*, their clear serious voices betraying the hold of that old-time religion. Cottonwood trees, candle wax, her brothers laughing in the backyard, her sisters snapping tea towels, her childhood dog snatching an ice cream cone from her hand. The future is their absence felt. As the youngest, she will likely be the last to go.

Her mom and dad are able to accept it all: the death of their parents, their siblings, their friends. Dollie will call Kerry to tell her that an octogenarian pal has had her driver's license revoked, a doctor Matt practiced with has golfed his last game, a family home has been sold and its contents auctioned off. Her mother will softly sigh, at peace with the inevitable.

To Kerry this news is jarring, particularly the stripping and selling of the family homes. With a Victorian mansion, or even a cottage from the thirties, this process seems natural. But a rancher built in the sixties, some suburban BC family pad that has been home to shag carpeting, avocado-green appliances, and Pudding in a Bag? It strikes Kerry that she has weirdly assumed that the places that have witnessed her history will somehow be exempt. The rain-rutted dwellings that have seen the evolution of wild western politics. The wood-paneled caverns filled with cigar smoke, pungent with beef slowly turning on the spit. Caves filled with newly wealthy men giving their past the finger, stoked to have beaten their way, starving, ferocious, out of the Depression, determined to slam the shiftless into action. Determined to run the commies out of town.

Despite their politics, their mindless, milky sexism, it devastates Kerry that those cowboys in leisure suits are now old or dead. That their tolerant women have followed, those lovely, cosseted servants in gold lamé hot pants, their hard dark lipstick possibly still embedded on the rims of a thousand martini glasses.

Matt hefts a leg over the baby gate at the top of the steep staircase leading up from the basement. "I'm going to have breakfast at that place where they give you the three eggs. Where's my angel, still in the sack?"

"Dad, don't… look, I'll show you how to open the gate."

Matt shoots her a fierce look. She knows that he sees her step over the gate all the time, usually juggling her laptop and a load of laundry. But the old man has forty years on her even if he is a powerful Mennonite farm boy who still skis in the avalanche zones. Kerry can't help it; she fears excessively for those she loves. Besides, she doesn't want to have to someday tell her daughter, *Grandpa died climbing over your baby gate, honey.* Of course, Matt would be down with that. He wants to go out with a big bang. No wasting away, no oxygen tanks, no toothless doddering. No time spent being spoon-fed. No time spent being useless.

"You guys need anything? Let me buy supper tonight."

"Sure, Dad, that'd be great."

He looks intently at Kerry for a moment. She wonders if he just noticed that his baby has a few strands of grey hair, the baby of all his babies is fading. She wishes she could spare him this cruel early morning view. It can't be easy.

Kat, stripped down to Elmo underpants, leaps into the kitchen stretching out her arms. "I'm a super squirrel, I fly!"

Kerry tackles Kat and tickles her daughter's belly. Kat screams with pleasure, "Stop, I-I-I'm a-a-a squirrel! Stop, Mommy!"

They tussle on the sticky kitchen floor until they are exhausted. Kerry blows a raspberry on Kat's stomach, extracting a final shriek, then looks up at her father. He stares down at them, a look on his face Kerry has not seen before, a look both raw and quiet. It's all there in the set of his mouth: he will not live to see Katerina become an adult.

"I know I haven't set the best example, but you guys should take that girl to church. Religion never hurt anyone."

Kerry laughs. "Jesus, Dad."

"What?"

"Oh, gee, I dunno. The Crusades, the choir boys, the car bombs—residential schools!"

Her father stares her down. Then slowly, as though speaking to a halfwit, he says, "It'll give her a moral compass."

"OK, we'll check out Buddhism, but don't be disappointed when the vegans show up for Christmas dinner."

Dollie emerges from the basement, her wisp-thin hair damp from the shower. Kerry's schizophrenic sister Lydia can't keep her hands off their mom's vulnerable little scalp. She runs her big raw mitts over Dollie's head, chanting *little wren, sweet little wren.* Their mother rears back from this, a head-shy horse petted and whipped by the same hand. Kerry must constantly fight the impulse to also be oppressively affectionate. Their mother's straight-ahead sweetness combined with a cool reserve has made even the so-called sane ones in the family crazed with devotion. Dollie is baffled by this neediness, this loosely reigned-in passion that rears up at the slightest opportunity. She fidgets with the baby gate. Kerry rushes over to open it. Dollie pushes her away. "I want to do it."

Kerry watches her mother struggle with the awkward wooden lever, determined. It strikes her that the gate is just as effective at keeping the seniors corralled as the toddlers. Diapers, walkers, baby gates—we all return to our infant state.

Matt pulls on his shoes in the small foyer. Kerry hovers, worried about him taking one of his long walks in this heat and smog. "If you want to try something different, there's a breakfast place just a few blocks north on Gerrard."

Matt squints at her. "You sure that's north?"

"The lake is south. Down south, up north." Kerry repeats her Toronto mantra, amazed to once again feel self-doubt creeping in. Her father can cause her to question her ability to form a sentence, operate a vehicle, a toaster. She knows he will do exactly the opposite of whatever she suggests.

"Do you want to look at that map again?" Kerry searches the sideboard, a once-elegant piece of furniture now a landing pad for bills, flyers, receipts, Kat's artwork, finger puppets, and a forgotten plate stuck with ancient crumbs. Her mother's home was crawling with children, yet it never descended into chaos. Kerry's sure her father must think that this is what she should be competent at, the smooth running of a pristine household. She grapples with the confusion of paper, desperate to unearth the map: proof that she is clever enough to find her way.

Kat blasts up and down the hallway in a small pedal car, laying on the horn. In the living room, *Dora the Explorer* bleats self-affirmations. Kerry turns off the television set. Kat wheels into the room, pulling up to the big screen in a rage. "I want, I want, *IIIIIIIwantttt!*" Her face swells red, she chokes on her words: such is the enormity of Kerry's crime.

"But sweetie, you weren't watching it."

Kat throws herself from the small car. She hammers her fists on the floor, screaming in pain and surprise. "My hands. I hurt!" Her wailing intensifies. She pounds her fists again and gyrates as if a thousand volts of electricity are slamming her small body.

Kerry sighs and sits down. "Is that working for you, Chicken?"

Dollie walks carefully into the living room. She places her hands on her knees and beams down at her frothing granddaughter. "Good morning, Sunshine."

"Mom*meeeeeeeeeeeeeeee.*"

Kerry crouches and opens her arms. "Come here, Sweetheart. Come here, Poodle."

Kat's eyes roll back. "I'm Katerina! I'm NOT POODLE." But she lets Kerry hold her and kiss her sweaty head.

Kat is peaceful now, using her mother and her grandmother as a human hammock, legs stretched out across mom, her head in grandma's lap. Kerry sips her espresso and holds it away from Kat's immaculate skin.

"So, being a former nurse and all, what do you think is worse for our sweet baby, the toxic smog or the radiation coming off the television set?"

Dollie gives Kerry a sad smile. "Oh, honey, Kat's fine."

"The crappy thing about being broke is you can't afford wooden toys. The good thing is the second-hand plastic ones have already off-gassed."

"Oh, you nut." Dollie shakes her head, likely wishing her daughter would talk about fashion, food, or anything that made a bit of sense.

Kerry wonders why she doesn't stop herself. Why torture her poor mother? Why inflict her dark, possibly insane thoughts on this sweet woman who has gone through so much and manages to live without bitterness? Her mom doesn't bother trying to save Kerry anymore. She doesn't throw the afterlife preserver into her daughter's murky swamp. They no longer have the conversation that ends with Kerry saying, "Don't you think I'd believe if I could? Don't you think I'd opt for simplicity, happiness?"

Kerry watches her mom run her fingers gently through Katerina's hair. Dollie's expression is tender. Her voice, when she speaks, is bright and delicate, like a snowflake. "So thick. Yes, you have pretty, pretty hair. Your mommy was bald until she was two."

"Does she really need to know that?"

Dollie laughs. "You had a sour-smelling head, but you were cute."

"Great, I reeked of yesterday's boiled cabbage."

"You were cute. You had that one dimple. Your dad is still so upset that he never had time to hold you. He loves babies. Always loved the babies."

"How could he not have had time to hold me?"

"Honey, we had so many of you, Dad was always studying and working at the hospital. He would be on night shift in Emergency for weeks at a time. He worked so hard for you guys; we rarely saw him. By the time he came up for air, you were already two years old."

"But still bald. I could have passed for a baby. Did he hold me then?"

Dollie smiles. "I'm sure he must have."

If Dollie was asked to write a scene-by-scene account of her life, she could probably do so. Not just the big strokes but the details, the colour, the texture. Kerry has been listening to her mother's stories for so long that they come to mind more readily than her own. Dollie's stories are achingly wholesome. She divulges nothing unseemly. Kerry suspects that when you follow the rules laid out by, say, Catholicism, you can probably give your life a nice, homely G-rating.

Her mother has only been privy to snapshots from Kerry's life—a life that if shown in full, would definitely be banned in many parts of the United States. Occasionally Kerry is tempted to blurt out some X-rated scenario from her past, some wild and filthy episode she can barely believe occurred. She searches for the point: to bond, to shock, to confirm that ditching religion at fourteen led to drugs, empty sex, and a tiresome load of angst? So, Kerry lets her mother do the revealing. She listens to the clean, well-worn stories in which even death has a happy ending, full of white light and loved ones.

They approach the Gardiner Expressway. Andrew is at the wheel, Matt is in the passenger seat, and Dollie and Kerry flank Katerina in the back. Kerry imagines her parents are somewhat relieved to be fleeing the big stinky city and heading back to their lush Fraser Valley. Wedged between the door of the small car and Kat's baby seat, Kerry feels appropriately straight-jacketed. The air outside is leaden and thick. Every so often an electronic billboard blinks: "Smog Warning!" When Kerry and Andrew first moved to Toronto, they'd laughed about how the signage was the moralistic voice of the province. A wagging finger to warn of drinking and driving, speeding, being a bad citizen. Kerry wanted to erect one that simply said, "And another thing…!"

The final drive to the airport is always disconcerting, and the older her parents get, the more oppressive are Kerry's emotions. Last chance to duke it out, last chance to thank her folks for having the devotion to make the long trip. Last chance to convey her conflicted love. If her father refrains from punching her buttons, if Kerry can lay off his, if they can steer clear of anything of interest, the trip will have been a success.

Dollie, wedged on the other side of the baby seat, holds her granddaughter's hand. She breaks the silence. "This reminds me of when I was pregnant with Teddy."

Kerry looks at her mother, wondering what about this situation could bring back Vancouver in the late fifties, her mom's then-young body heavy with her first child.

Matt drums his fingers on his thigh. "Those were good times. Great times."

"We had that little apartment, and we could walk to Granville Street. I couldn't afford to buy anything, but I loved looking in those windows." Dollie breathes deeply and slowly exhales, a small hum in the back of her throat.

Matt turns to look at his wife. It is a look Kerry has seen periodically over the years: her father slightly taken aback, as though he has been splashed with ice water and can suddenly see clearly. A look that says, I picked a winner; I did pretty damn good.

Her mom basks in this moment of intimacy. "Remember you had that crazy bet going with Reg over whose wife would be the first to give birth?"

Matt chuckles. "Twenty bucks."

Dollie smiles at Kerry. "Your dad won the bet. Iris gave birth an hour before me, but I had the boy!"

Kerry and Andrew exchange a look in the rear-view mirror. *And it was all going so well.*

At Pearson airport, Matt pushes the luggage cart briskly through the crowds. Kat charges past them, thrilled to see an escalator up ahead. Kerry chases her daughter, annoyed that a large wooden advertisement blocks the leg holes in the child seat of the cart. She grabs Kat just before she reaches the escalator, prompting a series of outraged shrieks.

She whispers in Katerina's ear, "If you're quiet until Grandma and Grandpa leave, we'll get you a treat."

Kat stops shrieking immediately, a quizzical look on her face. Kerry has read that using food as a reward can lead to an unhealthy relationship with it, but right now she is pretty much willing to hand out deep-fried baby Tylenol if it will stop the screaming.

She looks back to see Andrew unloading her parents' carry-on luggage from the cart. Dollie has a small suitcase. Matt has a bulging briefcase and a gym bag. Her father says something to Andrew that Kerry can't make out. Her mom gets a distressed look on her face. As they approach, she hears her father say, "That's not true; Mulroney was a great guy, better than the scandal, better than the Liberal dictatorship."

Andrew shoots the cart to the right so it nests inside of an abandoned one. "Yeah, great guy. He sold Pearson airport to his buddies, and when Chrétien cancelled the deal, we had to pay forty million bucks to Mulroney's cronies."

Matt snorts. "Well, I don't believe it. That's just bullshit drummed up by our socialist media. You kids are all brainwashed from piss-pot to grave."

Katerina runs over to her grandpa and holds her arms up. He smiles with delight, puts down his bags, and lifts his granddaughter. She wraps her arms around his neck and whispers, "I'm getting a treat!"

"You are, are you?" He puts his forehead against Kat's and closes his eyes. Dollie languidly strokes her granddaughter's spine. There is nothing but this for a long perfect moment as the four adults find ease in the reprieve from opinion: this window in the life of a human being when love is uncomplicated. When rage is quickly forgotten. When the truth is simple and painless.

Big-Snouted Dog

Chilliwack, BC, 1978

The big-snouted dog slides its long, wet tongue across the chip dip. Bobby DeGroot dunks his chip anyway. Kerry watches, appalled. Still, it's exciting to be in this filthy basement with the popular older kids.

She's afraid to speak, and she's had to pee for over an hour. Kerry glances at Barb, who leans on the arm of the sofa. *Lucky duck.* Kerry is stranded in the middle, forced to face the room straight on. Maybe Barb has to pee as well, but she's busy feigning interest in an Alice Cooper poster hanging on the wall—the "Dead Babies" one. Kerry tries to quietly clear her throat. Barb ignores her and fiddles with her mood ring—it's black. She forgot to take it off before she did the dishes. *I'm forever trapped in a grizzly mood*, she said. Kerry considers nudging her, but then they might start laughing—like in church—and have to stumble out of the room they weren't cool enough to enter in the first place.

Kerry isn't sure where to look. She watches a water drop form in the middle of a spreading stain on the ceiling. Above it, Wendy finally shuts off the shower. Wendy is Randy DeGroot's twin sister. Right before the DeGroots lost their pig farm, Wendy switched to a public elementary school. She switched just because she *wanted* to. Kerry worships her for having that kind of power. Randy stayed with the other farm kids at Sacred Heart, pretending he was still one of them.

Gonna go wash my hair, Wendy said earlier, much to Kerry and Barb's horror. Then she abandoned them in the roomful of unapproachables. Maybe she did it to teach them a lesson. Wendy's like that.

They *were* invited—sort of. Kerry and Barb showed up, and this time Wendy didn't make them leave. Wendy has pencil-thin eyebrows and a pie-shaped face. She also has very large breasts and is considered good looking by those who count—guys. Kerry's mother thinks Wendy is as plain as a post. She says that someday Kerry will feel sorry for Wendy, whose father drinks and lets her run wild, and whose mother ran off when the going got tough. Kerry has no breasts. She wishes she were Wendy.

Bobby sits on the other side of Kerry. Their legs touch. He hasn't looked at her since he sauntered into the room. Instead, he concentrates on the food that is spread out on the faded green velour footstool. The stool, like the rest of the room, is covered in black dog hair. Bobby eats smoked oysters right out of the tin, and when he finally does turn to speak to Kerry, his breath is thick with them. "Why don't you turn around and check the driveway for me?"

"Huh?" Kerry feels colour rush to her face.

Everybody in the room stares at her. Even Duncan, the shy guy sprouting a skinny moustache, snickers. Barb leans forward so that her dark curls obscure her face and squeezes Kerry's wrist.

Wendy leans in the basement doorway, smirking. She wears a pink childish nightie and pulls a fat comb through her thin wet hair. "Yeah, *check the driveway*, Kerry." Wendy winks at her brother.

To "check the driveway," Kerry has to turn around, kneel on the sofa, and look out the window. She wishes her jeans weren't so tight, or that she had a sweater tied around her waist. Somebody flicks a beer cap, and it grazes her thigh.

"No one's there."

"Keep checking," says Bobby.

A cigarette hisses as it's dropped into a bottle. Kerry's face is so hot, she presses her forehead against the glass to cool it down. She pretends she's in her basement at home. It smells clean. Her own sweet dog, Snicker, clicks her toenails across the floor. But it isn't Snicker who sticks her snout between Kerry's legs, shocking her back into the foreign basement.

Laughter.

"Bitch, come here, girl." Bobby rumples the dog's ears. "You a lezzie, huh, Bitch?"

Kerry flinches.

More laughter.

"Hey, you fuckin' heads, it's almost midnight." Wendy must be looking at the grandfather clock with the grease-smudged face.

Kerry turns away from the window and slips back into her seat. She is careful not to let any part of her body touch Bobby's. He moves closer and puts his arm on the back of the sofa.

"Ten, nine, *eh-yay-eight*," Wendy begins a heavy metal countdown to midnight. She leaps around and wags her tongue like Gene Simmons. Her nightie flies up to reveal stained underwear. Barb and Kerry look at each other and start to laugh. It's okay to crack up at Wendy's jokes. The underwear makes Kerry feel sad, though, but she keeps laughing, holding her stomach and leaning forward. Bobby crams his arm behind her. When she sits back again, it's there, a hard warm pillow.

Randy has been sitting cross-legged on the floor all night. He stares hard at his brother. Kerry glances at Bobby. He shoots Randy an icy smile. Since leaving Sacred Heart

Elementary School, Kerry and Randy have both changed. At the public junior high, they share a table in art class and the rank of outsider. They were sullen with each other at first, but now they hand each other charcoal, smudged fingers occasionally lingering. Randy should have gone to Sardis Senior Secondary, enjoyed farm boy status, and dated creamy-skinned milkmaids like Mary Anne Yonk. Instead, he's stuck in town, living in a shack on Railway Avenue. And like Kerry, he has hit the junior high cold. No ready-made public-school friends. No established personality.

"Midnight!" Wendy flies up and splays her legs while mime gripping an air guitar.

Kerry watches Duncan make his way around the room, surprisingly not too shy to take advantage of New Year's Eve. *He must have glugged back a lot of Jack Daniel's.* As Duncan finishes kissing each girl, they look disgusted and wipe their mouths. Kerry thinks they're just being cruel—Duncan isn't popular either. She smiles at him as he approaches. He doesn't really look at her, just dives for her face. Kerry gags on his ham-shank tongue as he drives it down her throat.

"Happy New Year," says Duncan and moves on to Barb.

As Kerry is about to wipe the spittle from her lips, her hand is grabbed in mid-air by Bobby. He jerks her toward him and opens his mouth. Bobby's kiss is dryer at least, a fish sucking at the air. Kerry endures it and tries to ignore the taste of second-hand oysters. Bobby doesn't stop kissing her. Kerry gently tries to pull away. She knows she's supposed to be flattered by his attention.

"Next party—Yeeooww!" Wendy runs out of the room, her bare feet pounding up the stairs as though she's wearing heavy boots.

Kerry can hear everyone dispersing, organising rides. She is still in Bobby's grip. He continues to suck. Her mouth feels too dry now—like she's being worked on by a dentist.

"Kerry?" Barb sounds worried.

Kerry roughly pulls herself away from Bobby, but he easily grabs her head and clamps back onto her mouth. She feels like she's being held under water. She can smell and hear the dog panting beside them.

"Kerry . . . let's go to the other party."

Bobby pushes his free hand down Kerry's pants and pops the top button off. The dog barks and scrapes her paw against Kerry's thigh.

"Let her go." Barb starts to cry.

Kerry thrashes out an arm in Barb's direction. Barb grabs it and starts to pull. For a moment, Kerry can breathe. She can also see the hateful expression on Bobby's face. He looks at Barb.

"Out, bitch."

The dog whimpers. Bobby laughs. "Yeah, you too, girl—get yer own date."

"Hey, moron—hey, dickless wonder." Randy stands in the doorway and holds a lighter underneath a signed Alice Cooper T-shirt.

"You wouldn't dare, worm."

Randy flicks the orange Bic, singeing the bottom of the shirt. Bobby leaps off the sofa, trips over the dog, and knocks the food off the footstool. Kerry can see that the oysters and dip will eventually fuse with the green shag carpet. The mould will probably match. Bobby scrambles to his feet and kicks at the dog.

"Run, Kerry. Run!" shouts Randy as he disappears around the corner.

Bobby falters. He looks at Kerry, stupefied. Then he tears after his brother.

Kerry is frozen. Furniture is being overturned upstairs. She can hear muffled shouting through the ceiling. Barb grabs Kerry's hand and anxiously leads her out of the house.

It's starting to snow again. They left without their coats, which were upstairs, slung over a kitchen chair. Kerry climbs behind a pitted slushy bank and pulls down her pants. "I have to pee so bad."

"I'll stand watch." Barb crosses her arms over her chest and looks down the road.

The streets are deserted, and Kerry is glad to have Barb standing there. She looks perfect. A fairy tale figure in a Make It Snow globe that someone has just given a good shake: Snow White, under the streetlamp, her thin ruby red sweater magically keeping her warm.

Kerry turns her face to the sky. Whisper-fine flakes land on her eyelids and cheeks.

Scentless.

White.

"Kerry," Barb whispers hoarsely.

Behind her, a snotty sneeze. Panting. The big-snouted dog has followed them. Kerry's teeth begin to chatter like they'll never stop.

Uncle Piotr

Edmonton, 1995

Uncle Piotr died a week ago. His life left in boxes, cupboards, trunks, desks, and scattered all over the floor. An ironing board stood in the kitchen with plates of half-eaten food on it; he had not wanted to clear off a table. Kerry and Dollie are especially saddened by the French fries in the cast iron pan, his last meal.

When Piotr had his second stroke, his landlord called Dollie. She immediately called Kerry.

"He stopped retrieving his mail six days ago," Dollie said. "The building manager finally entered the apartment with the master key; Piotr accused him of stealing!"

Kerry imagined her uncle in bed, his rich brown quilt pulled up to his chin, his eyes frantic.

"Stealing—*honestly*, Kerry." Dollie's voice sounded exhausted.

Kerry listened while Dollie talked about Piotr's escalating paranoia. Only once did her mother mention that before he died, her only sibling, her baby brother, refused to say goodbye. Dollie had phoned the hospital. "Do you want to talk to your sister?" she heard the nurse inquire.

"No, I do not," Piotr said defiantly.

Uncle Piotr had always been irked that Dollie never came to visit when the colours were right. Too early or too late, the leaves were either yellow or gone.

Kerry remembers this as she and her mother stand on Piotr's balcony, a fiery Alberta fall surrounding them.

"Oh, Piotr." His name sticks in Dollie's throat, giving it a froggy sound.

Kerry feels as though the little balcony is shrinking; soon they'll be standing on the width of a small board, teetering above the fires of Edmonton. Crisp leaves waiting to consume them.

The apartment buzzer sounds, Dollie scrambles off the balcony and rushes toward it. "It's Claire." She grabs the phone receiver off the wall. "Hello?"

Kerry takes the elevator down to meet her sister. When the lift doors open in the lobby, Kerry can see that Claire is still trapped outside, having a conversation with the intercom. They smile broadly when they see each other.

Kerry opens the lobby door. "Help meee," she says in a small voice like the one coming out of *The Fly* at the end of the original black and white version.

A crackling sound comes out of the speaker, followed by Dollie's voice. "This stupid thing."

"It's okay, Kerry's here," Claire says, laughing. Both sisters crack up. They laugh so hard they can barely drag Claire's bag through the door. Claire's mirth ceases immediately when she enters the lobby.

"It smells like Uncle Piotr."

Kerry lets the smell wash over her again. She holds Claire's hand as they stare at the elevator. They wait for their uncle to step out, grab Claire's bag, tell them how great they look. So excited to see them, he has their entire week planned.

"He's dead."

"I know."

Dollie looks tired. Older. Not her age yet but worn looking. Kerry doesn't want her mother to look her age, the age of Dollie's friends. The friends bent by bridge, booze, and blight. Some have even died. A few are like Dollie and their father, Matt: still skiing, still fixing a martini when they come down from the hill, still looking ahead. This is important to Kerry; she is frightened. Her uncle's death has left her mother unguarded. Only Dollie has the memories of her side of the family: the little brick store, the woman who made incredible Ukrainian meals and designed hats, the gentle father who died a month before his first grandchild was born.

Matt has ten siblings and most of those siblings have big families. His side is like a giant Pac Man eating the Ewaschuk side up. How can Dollie survive alone? No father, no mother, no brother. Kerry wants to protect her. Remember with her.

Piotr was a proud Ukrainian. A lover of jazz. A brilliant photographer. A failed real estate agent. An old bachelor. A grudge holder.

Next day, Kerry sorts through a drawer. She unearths a newspaper clipping about the Canadian comedy troupe, SCTV. The fact that SCTV had its humble beginnings in Edmonton is circled in red pen—several times. Kerry remembers an argument between Claire and Piotr. Claire had mentioned very casually that she thought SCTV began in Toronto. Piotr was furious. A year later, Claire had received a photocopy of this article—twice. Had Piotr forgotten he had sent it? Or, as Kerry suspected, had sending it twice been more satisfying?

As they dismantle Piotr's apartment, Dollie, Kerry and Claire take turns exclaiming from different rooms. "Oh, look at this, it must have been Grandma's."

Dollie tells them stories that they've never heard before. Unlike the stories of Sylvan Lake and dresses with princess collars, these stories aren't tidy. She tells them about Piotr's failed dreams. His inability to study—buckle down. His bad career choices. His jealousy. How proud he had been of her achievements—until Matt came along. For once, Dollie isn't presenting picture-perfect stories; she's picking through them looking for meaning.

Uncle Piotr was a flag-waving Albertan. Whenever he visited his sister's family in BC, he complained about the weather. "Shirt-sleeve weather in Edmonton when I left," Uncle Piotr would say, pointedly pulling on another sweater.

Kerry is neck deep in Uncle Piotr's history. Digging through the haphazard assortment of items reminds her of mining for treasures in Value Village. Her grandmother, Kate Ewaschuk, whom she is said to take after, is popping up in various boxes and trunks. Sad-eyed pictures of Jesus in ornate frames, meticulous hand-stitched tea towels. Kate was very artistic. She was a compulsive painter, changing rooms from deep pink to slate blue with her fluctuating moods. Kerry can relate to this aspect of her grandmother, but the pictures surprise her. With some guilt, she wraps them up for her own walls where they will hang next to a black and white framed picture of Charlie's Angels and a glow-in-the-dark Virgin Mary.

When Kerry discovered a hip forties-style raincoat at a second-hand store, she never associated it with death; someone had just tired of it. Now she knows she will always see death in the dispirited window displays. Death in the brightly coloured scarves and broken furniture.

Uncle Piotr suffered from heart trouble and unrequited love.

The official story is that religion played a part in Piotr not marrying. He was madly in love with a woman named Beatrice. They were engaged, but Grandma Ewaschuk disapproved. Dollie suspected that since Grandma was living with Piotr, she was afraid she would end up alone if he married. Beatrice was not a Catholic. Grandma Ewaschuk was *very* Catholic, particularly when her son was courting Beatrice.

Uncle Piotr had never seemed a pious man to Kerry. Spiritual longing maybe, religion never. He was a swinging bachelor who sold real estate. He had a panther theme in his bathroom, spanky nicknames for all his gal pals. Serious Catholic boys, as far as Kerry could recall, did not behave that way.

"I found the key," Dollie calls from Piotr's bedroom. Kerry puts down the religious icons and rushes to see what's hidden in the blue metal trunk. Dollie is kneeling in front of it, twisting the thin metal key in the big brass lock. Kerry sees her mother as a young girl, wanting to get at the secrecy of the trunk, the dress-up clothes it might contain. She pictures them on the cover of a Nancy Drew Mystery novel, *The Secret of The Blue Metal Trunk*. Dollie is becoming frustrated. Kerry takes over.

"Do you want me to do it?" Claire is standing behind them now. They bow to her competence and move aside. Quickly she opens the trunk. Inside they find half-used bottles of Rose Milk cream; dried up tubes of mascara and crumbly bits of purple eye shadow; unopened miniature bottles of champagne with poems attached.

"It's a shrine to a woman," says Kerry.

"Oh, Piotr . . ." Dollie sighs.

Claire is disappointed. To her, the trunk is only filled with garbage. She goes back to packing up the den.

"Mom, look." Kerry holds up a pair of purple polyester panties with a lacy edge.

"Well!" says Dollie.

"*Well, well, well!*" says Kerry.

The two women continue to dig through the trunk, pulling out more bottles of Rose Milk and several ladybug-themed items. Ladybug razors, ladybug oven mitts, ladybug candles. Kerry is tickled to find a ladybug phone. She lifts the receiver. "Who are you, ladybug?"

Dollie pulls out an envelope of photographs. The first is of a woman in her early fifties wearing glasses and a tangerine gown, tossing back a glass of wine. "It's Beatrice!" Dollie sounds troubled.

"The woman he didn't marry?"

"But, honey, *she* got married and had a family."

"I guess the ladybug didn't always 'fly away home'," says Kerry, digging through the rest of the photographs.

"They were just good friends when they were older," says Dollie, trying not to look at the pictures.

"Uh-huh, *look.*" Piotr and Beatrice snuggled together in the kitchen nook, legs entwined, faces glowing. They have set the camera on automatic. Beatrice wears the familiar flashy red bathrobe, Piotr an ornate silver smoking jacket. "Way to go, Uncle Piotr," says Kerry.

"Beatrice sometimes stayed with Piotr when she was in Edmonton. They went to the *theatre* together."

"It must have been an excellent performance the night before this picture was taken."

"Oh, you're just terrible, Kerry," says Dollie. "Well, I guess it's good he wasn't completely alone. He did say that Beatrice's husband was all wrong for her."

"Of course he did."

"You know, my mother could be a selfish woman sometimes. Piotr told me Beatrice wouldn't convert, and they couldn't get married; it was the *stupidest* thing." Dollie steals another glance at the photograph, her shoulders slump. "He didn't have to die alone."

Kerry fights the urge to straighten her mother's spine. Dollie is never defeated. Instead, she puts her arms around her. "It's okay," Kerry murmurs, rocking her; the soft smiling faces of Piotr and Beatrice look up at them from the floor.

Uncle Piotr became increasingly bitter. He was furious when he died, cutting everyone out of his will except for Kerry and Claire. He felt cheated. He was deaf. He was broke. He looked after his mother until she died; nobody looked after him. At the end of his life, only these two nieces squeaked in under the wire of his affection. *Just.*

Kerry and Claire go downstairs to use the apartment building's swimming pool and sauna. They are both remembering how they escaped their uncle on the last visit this way. In previous years, when he was in better health and humour, Piotr would swim with them. On the last visit he raged against: old friends, Matt's family, Dollie, waiters, cashiers, the young people moving into his building.

"Feeling guilty?" Kerry looks sideways at Claire as they hang up their towels.

"Extremely." Claire stops and looks more closely at her towel. "This is the same towel I used last year."

There is a silence before Claire's face scrunches up. Kerry strokes her back. "I know. It's hard." The two women go into the little sauna and weep in the heat. By the time they hit the water they feel empty and relieved. A row of big plants flanks a large window. The late afternoon sun lights them in a spectacular way.

"We should bring that big cactus of Uncle Piotr's down here," says Kerry, floating languidly at the edge of the pool.

"Maybe each plant represents someone who has died," whispers Claire. "It's sort of the obvious thing to do with a dead person's plant."

"Just when I'd found a place in the building that wasn't creepy. Thanks, Claire." Kerry is kidding, sort of.

Just then the door to the poolroom opens and an eighty-something-year-old man walks in. He smiles at the women and checks the pool temperature. They both stare at him until he leaves.

"He's good for at least a fig tree," says Kerry.

"I knew you would say that," says Claire, splashing her sister aggressively.

"Because you were thinking it too." Kerry allows her sister to splash her without retaliating. "Punish me, so I may sin again! That's as Catholic as I get."

It is day four in the apartment of death. Kerry and Claire have taken to calling it this, to bolster their courage, like laughing in a haunted house. He's still here thinks Kerry, his anger hangs in the air.

That evening, Dollie and Kerry drive Claire to the airport. She has to get back to Vancouver for work the next day. Claire has drawn them maps; how to find their way back from the airport and how to find Safeway to get more boxes.

"Getting lost is inevitable," says Kerry. "I don't know what alien fathered you, little Miss Sense of Direction!"

"She is amazing," says Dollie.

"You'll be okay with Kerry, Mom. You guys will be just fine."

"I'm afraid I might start laughing," Dollie says when she wakes up.

Kerry slept in Uncle Piotr's room with Dollie. This morning they are taking his ashes to the Catholic cemetery. A hearse is coming to pick them up.

"What?" Kerry is barely awake; they'd driven for hours trying to find their way home last night.

"Well, the funeral director has these hooded eyes," says Dollie.

"Oh, *no*, Mom." Kerry is filled with dread. Inappropriate laughter is another trait she has inherited from her parents. She rolls out of bed, naked.

"Where's your nightie, honey—honestly."

"I threw my T-shirt off—too hot." Kerry crosses the room and digs through Piotr's closet.

"Hey, it's the robe from the picture!" Kerry pulls on the silver smoking jacket and slips her hands into the pockets. Neatly folded in the right pocket is a small piece of paper. She crawls back into bed to show Dollie. In a woman's handwriting, in pale orange pencil crayon, are the words, "I love you."

Kerry and Dollie wait in the lobby. They are both dressed in neutral colours, unsure of how to look on this occasion. The real memorial will take place at Matt and Dollie's house in Chilliwack, but Piotr's ashes will be placed at the foot of Grandpa Ewaschuk's grave in his beloved Edmonton. Dollie is afraid to put Piotr with Grandma; they lived together for too long in this life.

"If I see a big, long hearse pull up, I'm going to start laughing," says Dollie, looking worried.

"Don't think about that, Mom; think of something sad. Think of Piotr."

A black Cadillac pulls up; a perky blonde woman in her early thirties wearing a smart black suit smiles at them from the passenger seat. Dollie and Kerry are so surprised they forget to laugh. Even when they slide into the luxurious back seat of the hearse, and Kerry is introduced to the man with the hooded eyes sitting at the wheel, they remain calm. They are transfixed by the unexpected woman.

Before going to the graveyard, they stop at the funeral home, so Dollie can sign some papers. Kerry is left alone in the car with the blonde woman.

"Are you the niece?" the woman softly inquires.

"Yes."

"He's at rest now," the woman reassures her.

There is a bit of a silence in which Kerry examines the woman's face. She is wearing thick pasty make-up. Kerry can feel sadness sneaking in. She doesn't want to cry in this hearse, with this woman in her death cosmetics and her tired, rehearsed phrases.

"Is this your career?" Kerry forces the focus away from her grief.

"Yes, I'll be receiving my mortician's license next week."

"I guess you've wanted to do this since you were a little girl?"

Little girl. Kerry sees her uncle photographing her as she feeds a pony through a fence.

Dollie and Kerry stand awkwardly beside the small deep hole that has been dug at the foot of Grandpa Ewaschuk's grave.

"I was afraid I'd be able to see my dad's coffin," whispers Dollie to Kerry. "I'm glad I can't."

The hood-eyed man and the blonde mortician use a well-practiced choreography to lift the urn out of the trunk and carry it over to the hole. They lower it down on something that looks like one of those Garden Weasels advertised on late night TV. Kerry tries to think about something else; she dares not look at Dollie.

The morticians leave them alone to say good-bye to Piotr. Dollie and Kerry look down the hole and at each other. They touch Grandma and Grandpa Ewaschuk's headstones. Dollie takes a picture of Kerry standing beside the graves. Kerry feels smiling would be inappropriate; in fact, taking the picture seems ludicrous.

Without ceremony, they are quite lost. "Good-bye, Piotr," murmurs Dollie to the hole.

Kerry is fingering something in her pocket. She kneels at the edge of the grave and takes out the note and the photograph of the lovers in the kitchen nook.

"Kerry." Dollie looks nervously back at the hearse.

"Please." Kerry hands an ornate lighter to Dollie. It is engraved with Piotr's initials.

Kerry holds the photograph and the note above Piotr's grave; Dollie sets fire to them. The note burns quickly. The photograph melts: Kerry lets go just before it burns her fingers.

THE GOOD LUCK DRESS

Math makes Kerry sick. Literally. She bends over her desk as another wave of pain hits. Mrs. Fonyo has just handed back her test. An F. "F." Fail. Fear. Father. Kerry's father will kill her. He won't care about the A in art or the B in English. Those just prove that he hasn't sired an idiot. Her mother was good at math. Her father was good at math. *She's not applying herself.*

Mrs. Fonyo is printing on the blackboard. A number line. Another dreaded, despicable number line. It's supposed to help with fractions. It doesn't. Kerry's friend Barb draws sinister versions of number lines and leaves them taped to Kerry's locker—like a skull and cross bones. It cracks her up. Not today though. Today, laughter is an ancient memory.

Kerry pulls herself out of her desk and staggers to the door.

"Sorry . . . bathroom."

Mrs. Fonyo looks at her with tender eyes. Mrs. Fonyo's eyes are so pale and milky she almost looks blind. They make Kerry want to cry. She wishes she lived with Mrs. Fonyo. Sweet old lady. Mr. Fonyo probably doesn't even exist. She's too kind to be under the influence of a Mr. Fonyo.

The hallway is quiet. Kerry puts one hand on the wall and keeps the other one on her screaming stomach. Mr.

Bradshaw steps out from a doorway as though he's been lurking there.

"Hello, Miss Wiebe."

Kerry nods at him and tries to smile. Usually, they clown around. He's cool as far as principals go. Except for his stupid joke every time she asks if she can borrow his phone. *As long as you bring it back!*

"Are you okay, Kerry?" Mr. Bradshaw is suddenly serious.

She can't answer him. She can't say *cramps*. And anyway, she doesn't get those yet. Her friends all complain—brag is more like it—about theirs. Cheryl is so pleased with herself; she'll ask for a *plug* right in front of guys. Kerry's mom hides everything to do with periods. *Men don't want to know about it,* she warns Kerry. Kerry suspects that her father does know about it, even if he doesn't want to, since he's a doctor. Anyway, cramps can't be as bad as big-math attacks.

Mr. Bradshaw won't let Kerry pass without an answer.

"Stomach," she says, turning red.

He smiles, thinking he understands and lets her go by.

The Ladies sign has a light inside. To Kerry, it always looks like the Ladies and Escorts sign at the back of The Empress Hotel. Her father makes her wait in the truck, underneath that sign, when she goes with him to pick up his native patients from up north in Bella Bella. They used to have their own hospital in Vedder, but the government closed it down. *Turned the goddamned Coqualeetza Hospital into a bloody rec. center, or some damn bullshit.* He gets the same way when he drives by the undeveloped fields on the reservation. *Just let it lie there*—bloody waste. Kerry expects him to lecture the men he picks up at the hotel. He never does. He asks them about their families. About hunting and fishing. He makes plans to visit Bella Bella again. Tells them if they take him fishing, he'll check everyone's hearing. He seems almost gentle. They call him Dr. Wiebe, but they say it like they're calling him Matt. Always a smile in their voice. Mock formality.

Cool, cool marble floor against her cheek. Kerry hugs her knees to her chest. Curled up on her side. Floating. She could drop her test in a puddle. Unreadable. And her report card—she could forge it. A lie. A sin. But still—he will kill her. It's only self-defense.

Zap. Another bolt of white-hot pain to the gut. All this, on a day when she wore her good luck dress. Well, no longer. Stupid dress. Stupid useless green plaid garbage bag of a dress. Kerry's pile of bad-luck clothing is growing at an alarming rate. Her mother is furious at her for not wearing about eighty percent of her wardrobe. She thinks Kerry is *just plain spoiled.* Once, Kerry took her mother's hand and led her to the closet. She carefully explained each disaster that had occurred as she held up a different article of clothing from the bad luck pile. Her mother sat down on the edge of the bed, her gaze focused somewhere beyond where Kerry was standing. Then she sighed and hunched forward as though the whole house had suddenly collapsed on top of her. Kerry looked at her slender back, thinking how her mom was never in a good mood when she wore her brown Wrangler pantsuit with the topstitching.

Kerry scrunches a corner of her dress in her fist as she lies on the floor. She will destroy it. Bury it in the backyard with the leather canoe wallets she lifted from Woolworth's. Bury it with the advertising flyers she never delivered. So much sin. Her soul is running out of real estate. Sister Virginia, Kerry's principal back in elementary school, told Kerry that every time she sinned, her white soul got a small black speck on it. Kerry isn't taught by nuns anymore, but she still tries to follow the rules. Kerry calculated a soul must be about the same size as an Oreo cookie—not a lot of space. The good news is she only has to go to confession to wipe it clean. And no matter how nasty the priest, God makes him keep your secrets. Anyway, she has to confess something, and it's too creepy to tell a man through a little window that you've touched yourself. She'll save all her black specs for that and just hope her soul has room. Some things are too great to sacrifice.

The door to the bathroom opens. *Please be Barb or Marley.*

"Kerry?" The soft voice of Mrs. Fonyo.

Kerry wonders if her good luck dress is riding up, exposing her underwear. She's too embarrassed to check. A hand is on her back, rubbing gently.

"Can you sit up, Kerry?"

Mrs. Fonyo's voice is so soothing that Kerry's stomach stops sparring.

She sits up. Tears are streaming. She concentrates on a piece of toilet paper lying underneath a stall. Mrs. Fonyo hugs her. She smells like fresh baked bread.

"Is it your father, Kerry? Are you worried about showing him your mark?"

Kerry's body starts trembling. Her teeth chatter. She thinks she must look like her dog, Snicker, shaking underneath the table during a thunderstorm.

"There now, come back to the classroom when you feel a bit better, okay, dear?"

Kerry nods, then sniffles, not wanting her to go.

After washing her face, Kerry returns to class. Nobody looks when she enters the room. It's as though they've been told not to. The dreaded test is still lying on her desk. Just seeing the sharp-edged paper makes her stomach tighten again. She approaches her desk slowly as though she's sneaking up on a snake. Squinting her eyes to make things go blurry, she looks at the mark again. It's a C—a C! "C." Calm. Christ. Crisis averted. She looks up at Mrs. Fonyo.

Her white hair has become a glowing halo. Kerry smiles and tugs gently at the hem of her good luck dress.

Pride of Alaska

Pacific Ocean, 1977

"All you need is a piece of the boner."

Kerry looks past Owen, the squat fiftyish steward, who has her pinned against the hull of the Pride of Alaska. She can see her friend Wendy who sits on a pillar of seagull-shit splattered wood and holds her head in her hands—her face zinc-white from puking over the side of the wharf.

Kerry snickers uncontrollably, even with wormy little Owen an inch from her face. She can't believe he said *boner*. Already she can picture herself slapping the strings on Becky's guitar (that she can't really play) and belting out "The Boner Song."

The Alaska Trip has been a big break for Kerry. Switching from Sacred Heart Elementary to A.D. Rundle—the badass junior high—has been harsh. Not at all the way she'd rehearsed it with her big sister Lydia.

Three years before, when Lydia was preparing to switch schools, they played a game. Kerry would pretend to be a cute guy who bumps into Lydia in the hall. Lydia would drop her books and bend down demurely to gather them. Kerry (cute guy) would bend down at the same time to help her, putting her face close to Lydia's. *Oh, oops . . . I'm Greg. Gee, your hair smells terrific.*

Lydia got dead-drunk at her first A.D. Rundle party. She was walked home by a boy named Reg, who shoved his hand down her pants on a shadowy corner. *His fingers were like dry knives,* Lydia told Kerry. Reg never talked to Lydia after that, except once—to call her a slut in front of his friends. That all happened before Lydia started acting crazy. Now Kerry is ashamed of her. It's hard enough to make friends at a new school without your sister dashing through a downpour with no shoes on yakking to herself.

Owen's round face is pink. *Pink Grapefruit Punch,* thinks Kerry. His head looks like a crackled tropical drink pitcher ready to burst. She wants to yell, *Hey, Kool-Aid!* Even his eyes are rabbit-tinted. Kerry isn't that afraid of him. He's older than her father, but not half as daunting—Owen couldn't give a crap about her marks. And yesterday, in that turd of a town they stopped at for an hour, Owen bootlegged for Kerry and her friends. Over-proof rum. They struck a match to a few drops and watched it burn. Friday night they're gonna swill the whole mess—mix it up with Dr. Pepper.

They're docked in Ocean Falls. The rest of the kids are at the fish factory—*retch.* The whole broken-down town smells fishy. Like the kitchen after Kerry's mom cooks salmon and has to light the big red cinnamon-scented candle.

Their teacher, Mr. Martin, said that Wendy didn't have to go to the fish factory because she had the flu. He asked for a volunteer to stay with her. Used to scrapping with her large family over a spot on the couch in front of the TV, Kerry was already mopping Wendy's forehead with her jean-jacket sleeve before another kid could even squeak. Mr. Martin looked a bit concerned. Since the Pride of Alaska left Vancouver Harbour, Kerry has turned from shy-girl into lurking chaos.

The reek of stale wharf merges with Owen's cologne—Hai Karate. Kerry recognises it from the time she dumped a sample bottle down her brother Jack's shirt, expecting him to become an instant Karate expert and jump-kick the house in half.

"Let's header, buddy." Donald, the tall steward with the Grecian Formula yellow crew cut, hisses as he walks by.

Owen reluctantly drops his arms and releases Kerry from her human cage. He runs a nicotine-coated tongue across his jagged chops and gives her a practised wink—too slow to be natural. Then he turns on his heel and the two men walk quickly toward town.

Kerry runs over to Wendy. They are both pretty excited. Wendy jerks her head at the ship. Kerry turns around and looks back at it. The quiet serious Captain stands and puffs Drum on the upper deck. He stares intently at the men until they are out of sight.

Kerry is almost fifteen and *still* as flat as a sidewalk. Wendy and most of the other girls at school have developed women's bodies. Their jeans fit them perfectly. Their T-shirts cling to baseball mounds. Kerry's mom bought her a training bra. It reminds Kerry of that carnival gag you see people walking around with at the town fair. A piece of stiff yellow rope fashioned as a leash, looped at one end around the neck of an invisible dog. Kerry's bra is pretending to keep her invisible breasts under control. At least when she wears it crumpled beneath her shirt it suggests *something* is going on. She refuses to stuff the cups with Kleenex. To be caught in such an act is unthinkable and she would be quickly exiled.

Kerry and Wendy kick around town—what there is of it. *We're travellers*, thinks Kerry. *We're in a foreign land.*

They find the one coffee shop. There is no blinking neon sign to announce it. In fact, it looks just like somebody's house. 'Ocean Falls Café' written in felt pen on the inside of a cut-out Captain Crunch box is stuck to the window and made waterproof with several pieces of wide yellowing tape.

When they enter, the busy cafe becomes quiet. Kerry feels her face heat up even though everyone must only be staring at Wendy. Kerry glances at her voluptuous friend. Wendy has a practised blank look on her face: eyes slightly lowered, mouth a fraction agape. Wendy slinks toward the closest empty table. Kerry follows her, feeling like the kid sister even though she's the same age.

A couple of young local boys saunter by slowly, smiling at Wendy. The cute one says hello. The other boy punches him—they start laughing. Wendy ignores them. Kerry smiles sheepishly, turning red again. The boys walk out the door and cruise by the window. The cute one waves. Wendy fiddles with her cutlery, checking her reflection in the knife.

"Thought you girls were sick." Owen's oily voice slides across the cafe.

Owen and Donald sit at the other end of the room, at a bare round plywood table. They sip amber liquid from juice glasses so worn they're foggy.

Wendy, facing Kerry, gives a sarcastic flutter of her heavily mascaraed lashes. Unable to be completely impolite, Kerry nods weakly at Owen. The waitress, a sixtyish woman wearing bright coral lipstick and a peach-coloured polyester pantsuit, shoots the men a warning glance before taking Wendy and Kerry's order.

"You gals like fish sticks?"

Wendy looks like she might puke again. Kerry orders for both of them. "Two orders of fries and gravy please."

"Fish sticks are the special."

"Uh, Wendy here is kinda sick—we're just going to take it easy with the food."

"Flu? She should have the pea soup."

Wendy bolts from the table. Before the waitress can explain where the washroom is, Wendy is outside, heaving over the porch railing.

Back in their boat cabin, Wendy and Kerry lie in separate bunks. Wendy, on the bottom bunk, fills out a quiz in a teen magazine. Above her, Kerry re-reads the orgy scene in *Once Is Not Enough*. She peeks over the edge of the bunk—hoping to take matters into her own hands. *Why won't Wendy fall asleep if she's so sick?*

Vicki saunters into the room, holding her nose.

"I shall never breathe again, *vile* fish factory!"

Vicki Stevens is tall with thick blonde hair that falls to her tiny waist. Her skin is pure satin. Vicki is the most beautiful girl Kerry has ever seen. Upon entering junior high, Vicki already had it made; even without her standout looks she would have inherited popularity from her big brother, Patrick Stevens. The family name is very important.

Kerry inherited disdain. The stigma of having a crazy sibling—she too might be off balance. And if that's not enough, Claire is a star athlete. Kerry has been a major disappointment to her gym teachers. She hates digging out her grimy gym strip from the top of her locker. Hates getting jabbed in the ribs during grass hockey. Hates the way the gym echoes with shouting voices and screeching runners. She especially hates the way she looks in her stretchy white shorts with her string-bean legs exposed.

Becky bangs on the door. "Hope you're decent, ladies."

Vicki and Wendy exchange a look. Vicki whispers, "You wanna get stoned?"

Wendy lowers her magazine. She pants with her tongue out and her eyes crossed. They all laugh.

"What a fucking head." Vicki twists her hair into a ponytail. "Just a sec, Beckereno."

Kerry swings her legs over the bunk. She wishes that Vicki had included her in the decision, but that will come. Already she's been invited to stay in their cabin—which is a top honour.

After they toast the joint, Kerry regales them with the boner and puke stories. She's always on when she smokes. And Vicki is definitely noticing Kerry's talent.

Becky reaches into her huge multi-coloured leather patchwork purse and pulls out a black plastic bong with a picture of a dope leaf on it. On some of the pale bits of her bag people have drawn things: the Keep On Trucking guy, Snoopy blowing a doobie on top of his dog house, and a happy face with jagged teeth and Becky's a *stoner* scrawled in blue pen. She inserts a joint into the cap of the bong, lights it, and screws it back on. After letting the bong fill, she squeezes it and pumps a jet of smoke.

Becky's five foot eight and close to two hundred pounds. She bought her way into the popular clique with drugs. Like Kerry, her wicked sense of humour also helped. Vicki is very fickle, though. And Kerry can see that Becky is nervous about Kerry's increasing acceptance.

"Open wide," says Becky maniacally.

Vicki obeys, flashing a couple of gold fillings inside her pretty pink mouth.

Becky bends over her, squeezing the bong slowly. A creamy white cloud shoots down Vicki's throat.

Vicki's green eyes water a bit. She doesn't cough. She's been a "professional smoker" for a couple of years.

Kerry knows she'll be last. Becky might even ignore her to make a point. She watches Becky move on to fluey Wendy, straddling her on the bunk.

"Christ, Becky, don't sit on my gut!"

They all howl at this. A perfect segue into Kerry's barf story.

They're ripped now: laughing and laughing. Kerry launches into the cafe barf story before Becky can shut her up with the bong. She imitates Wendy's retching sounds and describes people pushing away their fish sticks in disgust.

"I'm gonna fuckin' puke again, man." Wendy snorts as she laughs. It's important to make Wendy snort.

Vicki's laugh is somewhere between piano scales and exorcising a demon. Kerry is learning how to push Vicki over the edge—like tickling someone until they cry without touching them. Vicki commands Becky to fetch Kerry her guitar. Becky slits her eyes at Kerry, and her English-rose mouth puckers with rage.

"A piece, that's all you need," Kerry thwacks the guitar strings and sings like Dylan. "If you're pale, can't keep down yer feed—try a piece of the *boner*."

On *boner* everyone joins in singing, except Vicki who's laughing so hard she's flopping on the floor like a possessed Linda Blair. Becky sings louder than everyone else, trying to take some credit for the song. Vicki swats Becky's leg and between hysterical gasps tells her to shut up—she can't hear Kerry. Kerry is thrilled but fearful. Becky could crush her in more ways than one.

A knock on the door. Becky quickly shoves the bong in her purse and thrusts it under Wendy's bunk. Wendy grabs her magazine and skulks behind it, pretending to read. Vicki calmly takes a bottle of Charlie perfume off the dresser and sprays the room. Kerry, frozen, sits on Wendy's bunk with the guitar on her lap.

"Just a sec!" Vicki is all business as she opens the door. Mr. Martin stands excitedly in the entrance to the room.

"There's a school of dolphins outside, girls! Quickly now!"

Nobody in the tiny room budges. Wendy sinks further behind her magazine, muttering, "Big whoop."

"Be sure and give our regards to Flipper," says Becky in a honey-filled voice.

Vicki stifles a shriek of laughter, and a snort escapes Wendy. Kerry holds her breath; she's the only one who will face the wrath of a demon-father if she's caught smoking grass.

Mr. Martin, cheer snuffed out, smooths his fuchsia-coloured vest down over his slightly protruding belly and sniffs the air. "I hope you young ladies aren't foolish enough to become victims of the tobacco industry. Especially *you*, Miss Wiebe." Mr. Martin stares pointedly at Kerry. "Your father would certainly be able to tell you enough hospital horror stories."

"I had the smoke, Mr. Martin. Kerry doesn't touch tobacco," says Vicki, looking him straight in the eye.

Mr. Martin nods sadly. Vicki's mother lets her smoke at home.

Kerry is overwhelmed; *Vicki stuck up for her.* This changes everything.

That night, Kerry tosses on her skinny upper bunk. The Sacred Heart days are like a piece of garbage lying on the water, becoming smaller and smaller as the boat surges forward. Her dad has grey mixed in with his black hair, and her mom is going through mental-pause. She feels old. Change is a fat plastic chopstick jammed through her heart. Kerry and Janice no longer walk home from school together.

They were hanging out by "the tree" where the in-crowd smokes at lunchtime, when Wendy singled out Janice. She said, *Yer boyfriend drives a fish-wagon,* and I can smell you from here. Kerry wanted to smack Wendy for saying such stupid shit, but she jammed out. You can't have a crazy sister and stick up for an outsider.

Janice looked at Kerry when Wendy mouthed-off. She didn't even glance at Wendy, just stared at Kerry and waited.

Nothing.

Kerry opened her mouth, but her jaw just hung there. She felt like one of those in-bred kids from Columbia Creek that rides around like a big dog in the back of the family pick-up.

Janice didn't slug her. She didn't call her down. She just walked away, her shiny black braid swinging behind her.

Occasionally Kerry smiles at Janice in the hallway, but she ignores her. Kerry has joined ranks with Bernice Yonk and other useless bitches and the proud eyes of Janice Jimmie stare straight through her.

The next day, Vicki and Kerry stumble arm in arm around the outside deck. A frantic storm cuts across the sky, and the ship rocks like a bath toy. Kerry is having a difficult time walking anyway. She's wearing one of her shoes and one of Vicki's. Vicki's doing the same. They don't have the same sized feet—Vicki's are larger. Kerry keeps falling out of Vicki's shoe, but she's proud to be wearing it.

"I feel another chuck-fest coming on." Kerry stumbles backward as the boat is sharply tossed. Vicki titters and stabilises Kerry's slight body by grabbing her waist.

"Come on, stick-girl, let's sit in the nook and have a smoke."

The "nook" is a sheltered section of the outside deck. Kerry and Vicki dash for it as lightning slaps a white streak across the sky.

There's another passenger in the nook today. It's the heavy lady with the long greasy hair and dandruff the size of hail. Vicki scowls and pulls Kerry toward the other end of the bench—as far from the lady as possible. Kerry's had conversations with the lady before, her name's Jean. She knows that Jean has a sister in Kitimat and a brother in jail. Kerry says hello to her. Vicki elbows Kerry viciously in the ribs then pulls out her cigarettes. Kerry takes one, putting it awkwardly in her mouth. Vicki has a silver-plated Bic holder with her name sketchily engraved on it—a present from an older boyfriend who drives a Corvette. She cups her hand around the flame, lights Kerry's smoke and then her own. They exhale at the same time.

"My mother died from lung cancer. Bad way to go." Jean doesn't face them when she speaks; she looks out to sea.

"I'm sorry . . ." And Kerry is sorry. She painfully pictures her own mother dying. No longer existing.

"Gee, thanks, like we really want to hear about *that* right now." Vicki elbows Kerry again, much harder. Strike two.

Kerry's stomach rises into her throat. The boat tilts forward, then rights itself abruptly. She takes another drag, hoping the feeling will disappear. Jean looks directly at Kerry as the sky lights up again. Her mouth is pinched down on one side as though she was hooked like a fish and let go. Kerry drops the cigarette and grinds it under Vicki's loose shoe. She lurches to the ship rail and vomits.

The ship tilts again, throwing Kerry's small limp frame into the air. For a second she is caught in salty limbo, suspended between lead-grey sky and an ocean that looks like crumpled black garbage bags. Two strong arms pull her back to the deck. Jean crushes Kerry against her large soft body. Kerry can smell sour clothing and her own vomit. Lydia's ravaged face flashes inside her head. She wishes they were cuddled on the basement couch, watching *Love American Style* and sharing a milkshake. Kerry blubbers into Jean's chest. Missing Lydia, missing Janice.

Vicki, her perfect features all screwed up like she just swallowed some shit on a stick, yanks Kerry away. Kerry looks into Vicki's tough velvet eyes and shuts off her tears as easy as a garden hose.

She wipes her mind clean.

The Not-So-Secret, Secret Life of Angus McFee

Vancouver, 1995

Thu Jan 27 14:13:40 1995
Letter: 13489342 From: Moe@soft.com.ca
Subject AngusMcFee
Bytes: 245

Even from across this vast (&flavourful!) country I can tell McFee is up to something! Report back soonest! YES, Detective Wiebe—stalk the slippery sod! Somewhat sincerely, your deeply troubled and balding pal—who has no life because he's co-dependent and his reason for living is on tour. Moe "Fat" Shatenstein

"You're not sure which house he lives in?" Jen seems amazed.

Kerry bites the skin around her fingernail. Angus has been acting strange lately. Strange for Angus, who's not what you would call a regular guy in the first place. Angus likes his private life private. Kerry respects this—usually. When she left the house with Jen to walk to Canadian Tire, she had no intention of spying on him. Well, no *real* intention. She looks carefully at a house with a coral staircase and tentatively heads for it.

"I've only been here once. I surprised him. He didn't like it," Kerry says, reluctantly edging up the stairs. She balances uneasily on the top stair which is so shallow she'll be nose-to-nose with whoever opens the door. Jen stays at the bottom of the staircase, arms folded across her chest.

"You hang out with Angus every day, and you've been to his home *once*?" Jen shakes her head. "Weird."

"He has a secret girlfriend. I'm the ex, so he keeps us apart." Kerry knocks and backs away down one step.

The door opens. A woman with tired-looking eyes, long brown hair and glasses blinks out.

"Oh, uh, Debbie? Uh, I'm Kerry. Is Angus around?"

Debbie stares at her for a moment before saying anything. She looks amazed. "Right. Kerry. Yeah. I can't believe you dropped by." Debbie lets the door swing open further. A small sturdy girl of about five sits on a tricycle and solemnly stares out from the dark hallway.

"Redrum," mutters Kerry to Jen, thinking of the demented child in *The Shining*. Jen stifles a guffaw.

Kerry and Jen stand awkwardly. Debbie appears to be half ushering them inside the house. "Do you want to see the kids?"

"*Kids?*"

"I have a baby," Debbie announces. "Would you like to see *my* baby?"

Kerry and Jen exchange a look. It's like they've stepped into an urban myth, the one with the babysitter on acid who announces to the horrified parents that the roast is ready.

"*Would you like to see my baby?*"

Debbie's eyes are clear now and, Kerry thinks, almost too blue, like coloured contacts. Debbie bends down on the other side of the door and pops back up with a cool-faced baby, a baby with Angus's disdain already apparent.

Kerry sucks in her breath. "No way."

Debbie is smiling now. "Way."

Kerry fantasizes her reply to Moe's e-mail as she stands nervously next to Jen at the edge of Debbie's living room.

> Thu Jan 27 17:01:1995
> Letter: 23944567   From: Kerry_
> Wiebe@mindbend.bc.ca
> Subject MCFEE!
> Bytes: 70
>
>
> MCFEE HAS SECRET LUVCHILD!!!
> Sorry Fat, nothing else to report . . .
> Detective Wiebe

Jen and Kerry continue to hang back, like little girls who have been warned never to enter a stranger's house. Debbie thrusts the baby into Kerry's arms. On an end table is a big, flowered photo album. Debbie grabs it and brandishes it like a gun. Cracking the album open, and pointing so firmly that her fingertip turns red, Debbie proves paternity. Photos of Angus in a hospital gown, present for the birth. Angus bouncing his daughter on his knee with a squishy expression on his Leonard Cohen face. Kerry thinks that maybe she's in shock, and the baby could slide out of her hands; it *is* beginning to twist and wail. With a fierce expression, the mother stays bent over the photo album.

"Please, I believe you." Kerry hears her own voice falling like a leaf. Debbie firmly closes the album. The sticky plastic pages snap together.

When she reaches the bottom stair, Kerry turns to look up at Debbie who is standing in the doorway clutching her baby.

"Uh, congratulations." She can see that Debbie is starting to worry—Angus might be miffed.

Kerry and Jen wait until they are out of view before they speak to one another. Kerry realizes that this is absurd. To pretend that they wouldn't immediately put their heads together and dissect this soap opera is an obvious lie. An everyday socially acceptable lie, however—not like Angus's, which is more like a twisted leaving out.

"I can't believe he went to visit you in the Kootenays three days after the baby was born," says Jen, shaking her head and hands like she's trying to dislodge a spider. She's either as quiet as a shadow or as animated as a coke freak.

"Was it three days?" Kerry is purposely vague. She can't help protecting Angus.

"Are you going to talk to him? She said he's at the studio." Jen shivers again, "Yuck!"

"Yuck what?"

"Yuck. I'm part of this. I'm trapped in the web of this scenario." Hopping from road to curb, Jen starts her crazy dance again. "I was there when you got the big news, which means I will always be there!"

"Where were you when the secret child of Angus McFee was discovered?" says Kerry, laughing.

Canadian Tire looms in front of them, the parking lot filled with people who all seem to be dressed in the store uniform colours of brown and orange.

Kerry sighs. "That's one butt-ugly sight," she says.

"Go see Angus. You're three blocks away. You don't *really* want to shop for brake pads." Jen gives Kerry a small shove.

"Don't mess with my suit; you could be slapped." Kerry throws up her hands like a disgruntled Al Pacino character and swaggers off to confront Angus.

The doors to the warehouse studio are open, which surprises Kerry. Angus once had all his recording equipment stolen, including his twenty-four-track tape deck with a *nearly* ready-for-release CD on it. Kerry remembers the phone call; it was shortly after they broke up. She was seeing an actor; she thought she was in love. The pain in Angus's voice was palpable when he told her. "I came back from Seattle and everything was gone." He sounded like he was calling from a vast empty hall. The actor watched Kerry cradle the phone and sink to the floor. He raised his eyebrows in a parody of concern, and in a stage whisper asked, "Is it Angus?" How despicable the actor appeared in that moment, how insignificant. He was in a soap opera in L.A. for a while, a fact he feigned embarrassment about. Kerry imagined he saw himself in glorious close-up: knitted brow, penetrating stare, strong jaw. She turned away from him and tried to give comfort to Angus, her lips against the cold mouthpiece.

As Kerry walks through the door to the studio, she hears her own voice wailing in the recording room. Angus is remixing a song she did background vocals on. She hesitates under a shaft of light that pours down through the open trap door to the roof. Angus calls over top of her tragic soprano, "Kerry?" She moves into the dark mixing room and takes her usual chair.

"Debbie called. I guess the cat's out of the bag." He fiddles with a couple of knobs and puts a ghostly echo on Kerry's voice.

"Do I really have to provide my own soundtrack?"

Angus starts laughing the way Angus always laughs, open mouthed and silent.

"You are a complete psycho. You realize this, I hope." As she speaks, Kerry starts to laugh as well. She's laughing, only she doesn't feel like laughing—she feels like screaming.

As is their ritual, Angus offers to make a pot of tea. Kerry remembers watching *Perry Mason* reruns in their bedroom on Arbutus Street, drinking pot after pot of Red Rose. Since the medical study that linked black tea to Alzheimer's, Kerry and Angus have had an ongoing joke about his fading memory.

"So, I guess you just *forgot* you had a baby."

Angus opens his mouth wide. This show of big teeth confirms that he appreciates the reference. Kerry admires his teeth; it's a miracle they've survived his Scottish diet.

"Lose your memory you say? Pity!" Angus says this with a faux British accent as he dumps several heaping tablespoons of sugar into his teacup.

"You are such a weirdo!" Kerry rolls up the magazine on the table and whacks Angus across the shoulders with it. This is about as physical as they get these days; some unspoken rule has made touching taboo.

"What made you suddenly want a baby?"

"It wasn't my idea." Angus looks sheepish.

"But you went along with it—you agreed."

"She didn't care if I *agreed*, she wanted a baby." Angus shrugs.

Then Kerry notices that Angus is actually radiant. "Are you dazzled by your baby? Are you smitten with her?"

"Pretty much."

Kerry feels a fog descending, a mute anger.

Jen is outside the studio. On the walk home, Kerry's thoughts spill out. "I don't know what I'm feeling."

"Babies—weird. *Weird, weird, weird.*" Jen looks scratchy and tired, her manic phase passed.

"I feel, I *feel* like—a man can have a baby and keep it a secret for *four* months." Kerry rages, oblivious of Jen. "And still go to his bloody studio!"

"*You* don't want a baby, do you?"

"I don't know. Maybe."

"I don't get it. Don't get it. People having sex to create more people. Yuck!" Jen's voice is picking up speed again.

"What?" Kerry stops walking.

"It's completely illogical: there are too many people already, it changes your life, it changes your body, it's goofy. Yuck!" Jen marches on.

"How do you think you got here?" Kerry stares at Jen.

"Well, my mother didn't make a logical decision, obviously."

"*Logic*? You make obscure documentaries while living out of your gas-hogging, 70s Eldorado. I know poets who make more money than you!"

"Yeah?" Jen's voice is shrill. "Well, just try living out of your car with a greedy little *milksucker* hanging off of you!" On *milksucker* they fall down laughing, caught by the carpet of grass that runs beside the sidewalk.

"Yep," says Kerry in a crusty male voice. "That's a hell of an attractive little milksucker you've got yerself there."

"Hell of a milksucker," Jen agrees.

Kerry cradles an imaginary baby and they both admire its tiny hungry face.

Midnight. At last, Kerry is on her modem having a Real Time Chat with Moe in Toronto. Her screen is covered in question marks. Moe, code-name: Fat, is incredulous.

Fat: you're bullshiting me...ANGUS!!!!!?????!!!!!
Pusscat: i repeat angus has secret LUVchild--slackers oblivious.
Fat: I worked with himeveryday
ALLsummer!!!!!!?????!!!!
Pusscat: spare me the '!!!!!!?????' i know you're surprised
*Fat is laughing heartily

Pusscat: it's soooo weird
Fat: It's tooooo WEIRD
Pusscat: man who shares my brain...
Fat: sharer of my brain.
*Pusscat shakes her head in dismay.

Kerry and Moe have been friends for about six years. Their birthdays are on the same day, and their thoughts coincide like identical twins. Kerry dated Moe's ex-best friend Charles for a while. Charles used to beam at her and say, "It's like I've found Moe's personality in this little raven-haired rocket ship!" Kerry often wondered if Charles was really in love with Moe but simply found him too hairy. Moe was not big on that theory. "Pul-leeze!" he would say, "I'm trying to have lunch."

Fat: okay, let's s ay I believe you--with WHO????!!
Fat: ??!! oops...
Pusscat: with his GIRLFRIEND, debbie--the one he's lived with for FOUR years.
Fat: so now you're going to tell me she exists!
Pusscat: everyone says that 'with who' thing. Isn't the paternity usually in question?
Fat: Who knocked up Angus McFee?
Pusscat: Har har.
Fat: iguess you're going to throw a big shower.
Pusscat: everyone has already made that joke as well.
Fat: thankx for telling me last!

For years, Moe, Kerry and Angus met every other day for coffee and cheap laughs. They took over restaurants and small coffee houses, eventually finding fault with them all. The Slackers had big bright new plans every day. Then Moe fell in love and followed an actor to Toronto, leaving a trail of unfinished projects and an empty seat at the latest Slacker Cafe.

"She'll toast him," Angus reassured a moping Kerry.

"No," said Kerry. She sighed. "I think he's opted for one of those so-called real lives."

Pusscat: Moe... I miss you. Everything sucks.
Fat: Don't get all sloppy on me Kerry.
Pusscat: Angus is changing diapers, you're in TO and Jen is considering a full-time job. Tell me that doesn't SUCK?
Fat: Sounds as good as the weather here.
Pusscat: Dismal.
Fat: Dismal
Pusscat: Let's sign off while we're still sharing a brain.
Fat: Let's quit while we're one-head.
Pusscat: HAR!
Fat: Har, har.

Kerry disconnects from her Internet server. Her family and friends smile from where they are pinned and taped on every available surface around her computer. A much younger Angus, looking like a Scottish Bob Marley, poses in front of a warehouse that has since been leveled to create more parking spaces. Kerry sticks her tongue out at him. "Lunatic!" She climbs into her blue sleeping nook, which is large enough only for her futon and a wall-mounted bookshelf. She turns the ringer off on her phone. Propping herself up in bed with a giant floral pillow, Kerry prepares to paint her toenails. "Positively Pink!" she thinks, shaking the bottle. "That's gotta be me." When Kerry opens the bottle, the smell of old nail polish wafts over her. She sees her seven-year-old self, holding her short legs still while her mother applies a coat of red polish. Dollie's face beams up at her after she paints each toe. This image quickly dissolves into Kerry's grown-up toes looking at her from stirrups on a hospital bed, her chipped toenail polish an embarrassment. She feels like an ignorant whore. A cold doctor with a perfect blonde bob and gold studs in her ears slips something colder between her legs.

"Do you want to have this baby?" The doctor's voice is neutral; she could be asking if Kerry wants a mint.

"No, not right now, thanks," says Kerry. "Maybe another time."

Angus sits hunched in the waiting room. As Kerry approaches, he looks up at her. She shrugs at him and begins to cry.

Kerry screws the cap back on the nail polish. The terror of never painting a little girl's toenails overwhelms her. She's pretty sure there will never be another time.

Food-Combining

Kerry watches her father, Matt, about to carve the Christmas turkey. As a surgeon, he approaches the bird the same way he would a human body. He reaches for the gleaming silver carving set laid out for him by Dollie without a glance.

"Goodwill to Mankind, and more importantly, to me." Matt slices deftly into the Butterball with the tiny red pop-up thermometer.

"There wasn't an excess of goodwill towards that turkey," says Kerry, swirling the wine in her glass. "Call me paranoid, but I suspect it wasn't born with that plastic protrusion in its back."

Christmas dinner, 1994. Most of the Wiebe clan has gathered. The room is filled with the melancholy of unresolved slights. It's the first big gathering since the "War in the Woods," the massive protests over clear-cutting Clayoquot Sound. Kerry can feel the topic hovering over the table; she attempts to empty her mind by emptying her glass. An only-at-Christmas drinker, she repeats her inner mantra: *drugs and alcohol can get you through the holiday season.*

"Oh, Kerry, it's a *Butterball*," says Dollie, in her "Mrs. Matt Wiebe" voice.

"Meaning?"

"They inject the turkey with butter."

"Before or after they slaughter it?"

"Do you *mind?*" Kerry's brother Jack is already fed up.

"Oh, *you*. Anyway, the thermometer is just dandy, it pops up when the turkey's cooked."

Kerry snickers at her father who whistles while he carves the beast. She pictures him humming or singing in the operating room—a strong possibility. Kerry worked for her father when she was fourteen. It was her first job in an office. Before, she picked berries with her friends which meant mosquitoes, transistor radios, and for the chosen few (not Kerry), rumpled young boys smearing berries in their hair. The office had none of the smells or sounds of the berry field. It was the world of her father: deaf people, broken noses, office girls in pale pastel uniforms, an enforced hush broken by murmurs and typing. Then Matt would come crashing out of the examining room and shout a greeting to an old man waiting to see him. Or he would order Kerry to write down the lyrics of a song he wanted to memorize. When Kerry was told that she would be responsible for sterilizing the instruments, she was thrilled. Her instructions were to load them into a small machine, turn it on, and come back later and unload it. She was then to spread the instruments out on a metal table covered in cheesecloth. She proudly put each utensil in its specific place so that her father could reach for it mindlessly. Then she realized it was exactly like loading and clearing the dishwasher at home and laying out the carving set for the Christmas turkey.

"Goodwill to *Woman*kind," says her sister Claire, covering her glass with her hand as Dollie attempts to fill it.

"You're not having wine, Claire?" Dollie hovers the bottle over her glass.

"No, thanks." Claire picks up her girlfriend's hand and smiles at her. Maxie blushes. Dollie also blushes and looks away.

"Max won't be drinking *either*, Mom."

Dollie smiles weakly. It's an I-don't-have-to-know-everything smile.

"You guys don't drink?" Kerry's sister, Lydia, is warming up. Everyone in the room braces for the inevitable food-combining monologue.

Matt begins whistling the Christmas song, "What Child Is This?"

"Alcohol is so bad, especially with protein. I don't drink *at all* anymore." Lydia loads her plate with potatoes as she lectures, creating a miniature white volcano and covering it with cranberry lava. "You know, you really shouldn't eat potatoes with meat, like turkey is *meat* and potatoes are *starch*, and you shouldn't *even* be having them within hours of each other." Lydia digs into the side of the volcano and hefts her fork up to her mouth.

"I can't watch her eat," Claire whispers to Kerry.

Kerry is just glad Lydia's eating. Her beautiful middle sister got caught in the first wave of bulimia in the early seventies. Kerry remembers Lydia showing her how to stick her finger down her throat to make herself throw up. Kerry, a bone-rack, unaware of the purpose of throwing up dinner, tried it because her big sister obviously thought it was cool. Only Kerry was pushing her finger against the *outside* of her throat, which made Lydia laugh so hard, Kerry was glad she did it wrong. Lydia never showed Kerry how to do anything after that. The lively tomboy disappeared. Her clothes hung off her, her skin became yellow, her eyes dull. Soon she was medicated, taken away. Kerry was told her sister was a schizophrenic. Another strange medical term to get used to. Anorexia nervosa. Schizophrenia. Lydia.

Kerry feels her brother, Jack, watching her from across the table. He has an angry look on his face. He's focused on her T-shirt. She looks down. "STOP CLEAR CUTS." Kerry almost spits out her wine. *How did she do that?* She vaguely remembers dressing for dinner. She was going to put on her black dress. Claire came and sat on the bed while she was getting changed and handed her another glass of *glog*, a secret family recipe that smacks of over proof rum and cough syrup. Claire wasn't drinking, but that didn't stop her from aiding and abetting others. Kerry snagged her stockings on a jagged fingernail and gave up on her adult clothes. Claire threw her a T-shirt, and distracted, Kerry pulled it on without a second glance.

"Sorry, Jack, I had a bit too much glog today."

Jack stabs through a slice of turkey with his fork. The flatware skids on the china with a tiny screech. Kerry thinks she hears the bird let out a muffled cry.

Years ago, before she was an artist and Jack was a logger, Kerry would have been sitting on the same side of the table as her brother. They'd be laughing and talking, almost to the exclusion of everyone else. Kerry and her siblings would take turns impersonating their parents. Their world was small; Chilliwack *was* the globe. On those rare occasions when the family drove into The Big Smoke—Vancouver, Kerry was always amazed that the chaotic city even existed. All those people living lives that had nothing to do with Chilliwack. It hardly seemed possible. The city looked and smelled dirty, frightening, and glamorous. She finds it distressing that now the pollution from Vancouver drifts to the Fraser Valley, knocking down the sweet smell of cottonwoods and forcing asthmatics to remain indoors on fierce summer days.

"What's that green crap in the fridge?" Matt attempts to change the subject.

Kerry pretends that she doesn't hear her father. She tucks her napkin into the collar of her T-shirt so that only the letters ST and UTS show.

"What green stuff?" Lydia perks up again.

"I despise environmentalists," says Jack with a look that makes Kerry feel as though he's sizing her up for a chainsaw sculpture.

"What green stuff?" Lydia repeats. "Tell me what green stuff!"

"It's superfood, a vitamin-antioxidant mixture: spirulina, ginseng, gingko biloba extract, and about a hundred other things. It gives you a buzz without caffeine, keeps colds away . . . never mind." Kerry can't believe she's trying to explain her hippie health experiments while her father is in the room. She looks helplessly at Claire and Maxie. They both laugh.

"What a load of crap." Matt reaches for the sweet potato dish.

"All right, Matt. Just don't be like that," says Dollie.

"I take that stuff too!" Lydia interjects. "You know if you mix up your vitamins before you eat anything else, or you have them with fruit and eight glasses of purified water, you will be in perfect health. People are so *stupid*. Look at me, I got off that medication. I couldn't even *breathe* when I was eating all that meat." Lydia falters looking at the large helping of turkey on her plate. "I guess I'm cheating tonight because it's Christmas and everything."

"Tree huggers don't know a bloody thing about it," says Jack, red-faced.

"Would everybody calm down!" Dollie is close to tears. Ahead of schedule this year, the apex of their arguing usually coincides with the Christmas pudding.

"We have an important announcement to make." Claire and Maxie stand up.

"Who wants wine?" says Dollie in an edgy sing-song voice reminiscent of an 80s Trident gum commercial.

"I do."

"I do . . ."
"I do!"

To Kerry, Claire seemed so quiet when she was growing up. Her older sister with the long wavy hair and the sweet face. Remote. Friendly, but far away. Kerry later learned that Claire was weighed down with a secret and couldn't risk intimacy. Kerry was twenty-one when Claire came out to her. She had made tea, and was sitting across the table from Claire, waiting for her to put into words what she already knew. Claire was having a horrible time, starting and stopping and shaking her head. Kerry pushed the homogenized milk container toward her. They looked at the container, and then at each other, breaking into hysterical laughter. "Come out, come out, wherever you are," said Kerry finally. That was when their relationship really began. Sisters at last.

"We're pregnant!" Claire is holding up a glass of water.

Kerry, prepared yet not prepared for the nature of the announcement, springs to her feet. She slams her wine glass into Claire's so enthusiastically that they almost smash.

"Jesus H. Murphy!" says Matt, a look of confusion and disgust on his face.

"Which one of you is pregnant?" Jack has apparently forgotten Claire's recent hysterectomy.

"You know what, if you eat too much garlic when you're pregnant, your baby will be born aggressive. Parsley's good though." Lydia helps herself to more turkey.

For once Dollie is at a loss for words. She sighs and sighs and sighs again.

"A little aggression is okay with me," says Maxie.

"Especially if it's a girl—pass the garlic!" Claire tries to get Dollie to clink glasses.

Dollie raises her glass an inch off the table. She stares straight through Claire as they toast.

"To the baby!" shouts Kerry.

"Pass the cranberry sauce, please," says Lydia, her attention returning to her plate.

After dinner, Kerry is in the kitchen scraping dishes; Claire is rummaging through the liquor cabinet.

"Shouldn't you get married before bringing a child into the world?"

"We would if we could," says Claire, her head almost inside the cupboard. "I've been trying to support Max in the no drinking thing, but . . ." Claire finds what she's looking for—Irish whiskey.

"Just don't sip it in front of Max and make little moaning noises," says Kerry.

Jack awkwardly enters the kitchen, carrying his dish. He scrapes the remnants of food into the garbage pail, avoiding looking at Kerry. The men in the family have generally exempted themselves from kitchen responsibilities. Kerry can see that Jack is making an effort. She feels the glog in her stomach pitch.

"I'm sorry, Jack . . . it wasn't intentional."

"How could it not be intentional?" Jack shrugs; his anger has become something more familiar—distance.

"Excited about being an uncle?" asks Claire, bolstered by the whiskey.

"Well, yeah, I kind of am," says Jack.

Maxie runs in from the dining room. "Thanks for leaving me with the proud grandparents and the nutritional expert."

"Can I ask how you guys did this—I mean who's the father?" says Jack.

Kerry pulls the turkey baster out of the sink and rinses it elaborately.

"Kerry!" Claire looks nervously at Jack.

"Handsome devil … and so handy!" Kerry plunges the baster back beneath the suds.

"Come on, kids. Your mother wants to light the Christmas pudding," Matt calls from the other room.

Claire, Maxie, and Jack have retreated to the dining room. In the kitchen, Dollie is splashing Brandy on the Christmas pudding, and Kerry is lining up coffee cups.

"Shouldn't I serve coffee before you light that?"

"Oh, *Hell's bells,* I don't care." Dollie stops splashing the brandy and readjusts the sprig of holly on top of the pudding. The holly pricks her thumb, which begins to bleed. She sucks on it.

"Mom, I know you *do* care, it's going to be great."

"Great? What am I supposed to tell all my friends?"

"Say: I've got a grandchild, and you don't, nyah, nyah, nyah, nyah."

Dollie considers this, her thumb in her mouth.

Kerry fills the coffee cups, thinking about what has transpired. It's probably good that her sister isn't the one having the child. With the diversity that sprang from their mother's womb, it would be too much of a wild card. What would Claire do if she had to raise a child like Lydia?

Lydia wanders into the kitchen carrying her plate, trying to hide the turkey bones as she walks past Kerry.

"No turkey, huh . . . good for you." Lydia gives Kerry a sheepish sideways smile. "I wouldn't have except, well it *is* Christmas, and you know. It sure tasted good."

"You're allowed to eat turkey if you want to eat turkey, Sweetie. You're allowed to eat anything you want."

"Can I see your green stuff?"

"Sure."

"We're smart, huh, Kerry. We know how to look after ourselves."

"Yeah, except I'm not feeling too great, Lydia, I … uh, just have to go to the bathroom. I'll be right back."

In the upstairs bathroom is a magazine rack. Kerry can see the cover of *Metropolitan Home* through bleary eyes. The little bathroom has seen a fair bit of vomiting in its day. Her mother with her pregnancies, the kids with their flus, the teenagers sick on jars of mixed alcohol—"porch crawler." Lydia, when she suffered from bulimia: and now, adult Kerry, hanging over the toilet on Christmas night, ridding her body of toxic glug.

"Kerry, you're missing all the fun!" Dollie yells from the bottom of the stairs.

Ashen faced, and wearing a fresh slogan-free T-shirt, Kerry again takes her place at the dinner table.

Matt raises his eyebrows at her. "You smell like you just drank a bottle of mouthwash."

"I *feel* like I just drank a bottle of mouthwash."

Around the corner comes Dollie with the flaming Christmas pudding. Everyone cheers and claps. Behind her walks Jack carrying a tray of coffee mugs.

"Hey, Jack, you're pretty good at that," Maxie teases him.

"Are those still warm?" asks Kerry.

"I nuked them."

"Jack, you *are* good at this." Kerry almost reaches for her wine again, thinks better of it, and reaches for a coffee mug instead. Dollie slices the Christmas pudding and passes it around.

"I really shouldn't have any of this," says Lydia, snapping up the largest piece.

"It's Christmas, Lydia, go crazy, I mean . . . you might as well."

"That's right, it's Christmas! May there be peace on earth," says Dollie wistfully.

Matt makes a grab for his slice of the pudding. He holds the jiggly substance underneath his nose and inhales deeply. "This would be perfect with a mug of dark beer."

"Oh, Matt, that's terrible," says Dollie.

"I don't think that's proper food combining, Dad," says Kerry.

Lydia perks up. Kerry realizes she said the wrong thing.

"Did I mention that alcohol is really, *really* bad for you? It depletes your vitamins, dehydrates you, overworks your liver, and all that sugar, *sugar's the worst . . .*"

Distance

Edmonton, 1993

Riding shotgun in her uncle's 1990 Subaru Outback, Kerry leans forward to grip the two front seats. A grinding whine fills the car as Uncle Piotr guns the pedal to the metal in first gear. From the passenger side, Claire anxiously points at the oncoming traffic. She starts to say something and stops.

Uncle Piotr isn't really looking at the road—he's transfixed, staring at snapshots that run like a storyboard across the inside of his head. Right now, he's enjoying Dancing Kerry, age ten. She wears a Ukrainian headdress and kicky red shoes: *Saucy Sues.* He knows that's the brand name because Dollie told him at least seventeen times, and he thought it was damn cute. He'd feign surprise every time Dollie said, "Oh, those Saucy Sues!" But the fresh delight was real enough. He almost grins at this memory when Claire's fluttery hand lands on his shoulder and startles him back into the horrible now. From behind him, the cocky voice of grown-up Kerry seals it. "Whoa there, Uncle P." Uncle Piotr glares at the world and shifts out of first; the car lurches as though shot from a sling.

They drive in hawkish silence until Uncle Piotr can't take it anymore and lobs a fresh bomb. "It makes me *so blame mad!* These single and *whatnot* mothers teaching their little boys how to do the dishes!"

The sisters exchange a look: Claire makes tiny "no" motions with her head while Kerry mimes blowing her own brains out with a gun to the mouth. They have come to spend a week with their uncle in Edmonton. His sister is concerned about him.

"He's mad at everybody!" Dollie warned them. "Don't disagree with him if you can help it."

He is very angry at Dollie, which is why she has sent her daughters.

Kerry is already bored with biting her tongue. Even the back of her uncle's head is beginning to look smug: tufts of white hair outlining the shiny spotted surface like a crop circle. He nods as he talks, as though by physically agreeing with himself he can persuade them as well.

Uncle Piotr is expounding on his favorite topic—*girls are girls and men are men*. "Boys can mow the lawn, pull their weight that way . . . that's just great!" Uncle Piotr relaxes as though he has hit the vein of reason.

"So, I guess the fellas get the entire winter off then?"

"Kerry . . ." Claire sounds nervous.

"If I ever do reproduce, *and* it's a boy, he'll be baking tofu quiche while washing the floor with his left foot by the time he's twelve!"

"Uncle Piotr, *you* never married," says Claire gently. "You've had to acquire domestic skills yourself, so why would you object to instructing a child—" She is cut off by a loud *shreee* sound as Uncle Piotr adjusts his hearing aid.

"If the boy grows up and marries a career woman, then okay." Uncle Piotr pauses.

"Okay *what?*"

"Okay, if husband and wife are both working, then *sure*, he can always learn." Uncle Piotr grinds another gear.

Kerry smacks her forehead. "Why can't he pick up this information in his formative years? Why does it have to be a bloody miracle that young Biff knows what a tea towel is?"

The car putters through a red light, silencing Kerry and Claire. They hold hands between the front seat arm rest. Claire whispers, "Let it go, or we're all toast." The other cars simply wait. They don't lean on their horns like people would in Vancouver or Toronto. Remarkably, here in Edmonton, they take it in stride. Kerry remembers watching a documentary about seniors losing their driving skills. One woman coasted into a crowd of people, then drove through the side of Woodward's department store with six pedestrians plastered to the hood of her car. The argument is over, Kerry searches for her seat belt.

That night the sisters decamp to the guest bedroom. They vacillate between fury and guilt. In Kerry's journal, each day is ticked off prison style: *Lest we lose our minds and all sense of time*. It's as though the uncle they had adored as children, the laughing bachelor who wrapped their gifts in polka dot paper, has morphed into an oppressor and taken them hostage in his overheated apartment. He fattens them with perogies and sour cream. Activities beyond the interior of the building or the inside of his car feel forbidden. To enter and leave the complex, they have to take an elevator to and from the underground parking garage—although Kerry has gone rogue twice to hike the twenty flights of stairs. Roadside attractions are ignored when they go out for supplies—they only ever stop at malls with underground parking.

"It's almost crueler to have windows." Kerry looks wistfully out at the lights of Edmonton. "Especially when they're painted shut."

The sisters sit up in the double bed, their pillows propped against the elaborate satin headboard. Both are attempting to read themselves to sleep, but the sound of the heat kicking in makes them sigh in unison.

"I know there are worse things in life—I just can't remember what they are right now."

"It's day four," Claire reminds her. "We can do this thing!"

Kerry fans herself with the thick leather-bound collection of Jane Austen novels she has pulled from her uncle's shelf. "Jane isn't helping. I feel like I should rescue her—would he notice she was gone?"

"Yes." Claire pats Kerry's arm and turns her attention back to her book.

Kerry surveys the room papered with the past: a picture of Dollie smiles from the wall. She holds a bouquet of roses, her nurse's cap a halo on perfect cherub curls. On the dresser, Ukrainian Easter eggs fill a dusty bowl next to a red plastic head that bounces if you tap it, like it's chortling at some private joke.

"The phone never rings," says Claire sadly, not looking up.

Kerry reaches for her mug of NeoCitran and takes a sip. She claims it's for her allergies, but really, it's to deaden her insomnia. She makes a feedback sound in Claire's ear, "Shreeeee."

They laugh, cover their mouths, and kick their feet. "We're going to Hell," Claire sputters. Kerry knows that she alone will be going to hell if the ticket price is irreverence. Claire is too kind, has too much of the angel on the bureau in her nature.

Kerry awakes to find she has all the covers and is sprawled in the center of the bed. Claire must have risen early. She smells kolbassa cooking and hears muted conversation coming from the other room. "I am going to be nice today!" Kerry promises aloud.

Groggy, she enters the kitchen. Claire is finishing her breakfast at the table.

"Good morning, Cupcake," says Uncle Piotr, pulling back a chair. "Ah, she found the house coat!" He seems pleased that Kerry is wearing the flashy red robe provided for female houseguests.

Uncle Piotr has set a place for her, excited to serve the traditional sausage of the Ukraine. Kerry flinches. To remind her uncle that she doesn't eat meat would dash this moment to pieces. "Wow, that does smell amazing. I, uh, I'm really tempted."

The smell of meat hangs in the air, familiar, simple: a soft curtain dotted with hunters taking aim while trusty dogs flush grouse from the brush. Uncle Piotr smiles as he loads her plate. Kerry wants to cry: for not getting married, for not wearing panty hose, for disappointing everyone and not being a Cupcake.

She puts a piece of kolbassa in her mouth. As she bites down, the skin pops in a spray of warm fat. She remembers a made-for-television movie called *The Sin Eater*. In the final scene, the son of the Sin Eater is faced with his father's corpse laid out in white robes, the centerpiece to a sumptuous buffet. The boy is expected to eat all the food, thus cleansing his father's soul. Kerry was twelve when she watched it, and until now, she had not understood why the boy was wailing while he ate his father's sins, unable to divert his destiny.

Kerry watches as Claire clears away her breakfast dish and finds a piece of partially chewed kolbassa hidden beneath a tomato slice. Claire grins at her and discreetly scrapes it into the garbage.

Evening. Kerry sets up her video camera. Uncle Piotr is going to show them old photographs. As she fiddles with the camera, Kerry can feel Uncle Piotr eyeing it suspiciously. To make matters worse, she is having trouble adjusting the tripod.

"Come and sit down, Cupcake," he orders, patting the Harvest Gold kitchenette chair.

"I really want to film this," says Kerry, finally thrusting the camera into place. "It'd be great if you'd hold the photos up to the camera."

The red light comes on. Piotr, a hobby photographer, calculates what the camera is seeing and edges his body out of frame so that only his hands can be recorded as they sort pictures.

"Oh, that's interesting," Kerry laughs tersely. "New Ukrainian Cinema."

"New what, Cupcake?" asks Piotr, his hands hesitating on a photo that shows Piotr and Dollie, arms around each other, on a wharf at Sylvan Lake.

"New Ukrainian Cinema . . . the next wave."

"What's new?" Piotr asks again, tracing the wharf with a sad finger.

"Nothing. Nothing's new."

The next morning, they go for a drive in the Alberta countryside. Kerry feels slightly nauseous from filming the flat oppressive beauty out the car window. To Kerry, the oil rigs look like sci-fi creatures—half dinosaur, half machine—sucking the moisture out of the earth. A car passes with a skeletal-faced man rigid at the wheel. His image blurs as the camera auto-focuses. Kerry pulls the camera away from her eye in time to see an ancient, weathered Reform Party sticker half peeled from his bumper. Up in the front seat, Claire is making "nice" conversation. Since the third red-light encounter, the sisters have decided to lower their individual odds by time-sharing the Death Seat.

"Keep conversation to a minimum, Claire. He can't read our lips and drive at the same time," Kerry half-joked before they left the apartment.

They pass a large sign for Taber Corn.

"Is Taber a town?" asks Claire politely.

Uncle Piotr looks straight at her as he leans half out of the driver's seat towards Claire. "What, Sweetie?"

Claire raises her voice, "Taber corn. *Corn.*"

He leans closer yet, the car's right-side drifting onto the shoulder, "You want some corn?"

Kerry pictures the three of them in a gruesome tangle of metal. She shudders, then titters uncontrollably, pulls her hair and sticks a fist in her mouth. Claire reaches between the seats and pinches her leg hard. "No, Taber . . . forget it."

A painful expression flashes briefly across Piotr's face.

Twenty minutes later, released from the confines of the car, the sisters bolt like unleashed dogs. "Yes, yes, *yes,*" cries Kerry, hugging her camera and lapping up the fresh air. Claire stops herself and falls back to keep pace with Uncle Piotr. Kerry turns around and walks backward, filming Piotr and Claire wandering on the riverbank.

Piotr realizes Kerry is filming and ducks behind Claire. He stops to fiddle with his shoe and waves Claire forward. He watches her sprint towards her sister. She takes the camera from Kerry and begins filming her. Kerry seems to be pretending to be a reporter. Her big boots are nearly as cheeky as she is. Piotr wishes she wouldn't bother wearing dresses if she has to wear army boots with them. He feels a creeping anger and sits down to make it apparent that he is tired.

Kerry is dancing now while Claire films, laughing and jiggling the camera. Piotr looks on, wondering what is *so blame funny*. It's not as though he can tease his sister's kids. Just like their father, no humour. He ponders this, no *good* humour. He thinks about his sister. Dollie married a doctor, went on her honeymoon and never returned. A woman came back with her red smile and slight body, her oddly stubby thumbs that she used to flash like a secret code. But like someone who discovered religion, the changes were below the skin. Certain jokes felt off limits. She wouldn't sit down with her coffee anymore. She couldn't stop wiping the table. She was keeping the great doctor's home. Dollie. Dollie who played the violin, wrote brilliant essays, took little Piotr to the library on Sundays and then for a malted at the Bay. His big sister. His.

"Are you tired, Uncle Piotr?" Claire's kind face looks worried.

Piotr hears the word "tired." Possibly. To him it sounds like *A Rutiffered UnCLee?* I'd like to repeat this nonsense back to her, he thinks. *Noo, I'm rallly godmifff!* He can see that Claire moves her lips very purposefully, that she is trying. He smiles, covering his contempt. Sweet Claire, he still shudders to think that she is a lesbian, although with Matt Wiebe for a father he can understand why she hates men. She once told him that she didn't hate men—she just loved *women.* Now *that* made his skin crawl. Even the affection between the sisters is getting to him. Kerry constantly throwing her arm around Claire in public, hugging her, calling her Apple Head. Kerry with her big boots and spiky hair, anyone looking over would think, 'Dykes!' Piotr Ewaschuk was *related* to these "Women Who Would Never Be Mothers." Oh, Kerry had always had boyfriends. He'd never forget that asshole Angus, bloody communist. Imagine calling Northlands Coliseum a monument to fascism! At least Angus was out of the picture, even if Kerry still maintained a close friendship with him. *Still friends.* What a ridiculous generation. Underneath his liberal facade, his commie, free-love bullshit, Angus must think

Kerry a fool. She hands over her body so lightly, for no return. Her body so like Dollie's.

"What are you thinking so deeply about, Uncle P?" Kerry has that bloody camera pointed at him again. To his chagrin, he finds her easier to understand than most people.

"Oh, just how cute you two gals are."

Kerry smiles a genuine smile and Piotr feels his irritation rise again. "Too bad they didn't give you back your shoes when you quit the army."

"Too bad they took away my big gun," says Kerry, her face darkening.

"I love her boots, Uncle Piotr," says Claire defensively, putting her arms around Kerry from behind.

"Extreme close-up of a bogman." Kerry zooms in on Piotr's face.

"Pardon, Cupcake?" He adjusts his hearing aid, twisting it until it shrieks. She says nothing.

"You kids sure don't like being teased!" Piotr gloats. "Your mom and I had a lot of laughs. Oh well, I guess it's the rare few."

That evening the sisters escape to the sauna in the basement of the apartment building. Kerry throws the racy red robe on the floor. "If he implies one more time that we're humour deficient because we don't laugh at his bad puns and pointed jokes, I might have to hit him."

"He asked every cashier to smile today," says Claire, her toe prodding the robe where it lies like a bloodstain. "It was horrible."

"Oh, God," Kerry winces. "He kept pulling the old if-there's-no-price-on-it-I-guess-it's-free routine."

"They did smile though. Mostly."

"Because that's what women are trained to do," says Kerry crisply. "We smile on command."

Kerry recalls herself at nineteen, working at the liquor store. "I guess you'll be wanting my ID there, eh, miss?" the old daily-drinkers would always say.

"You didn't get that veiny beak drinking Kool-Aid," she fantasized replying. Yet she knew that they were only trying to conjure up warmth, a friendly familiar exchange, and she always played along. She smiled.

The sisters lean on opposite walls. The sauna has made their skin pink. Kerry opens one eye and looks at Claire whose jaw is tightly set.

"Relax," says Kerry. "Let those toxins go!"

Claire's hand moves to the healing scar on her belly. "It's massive, isn't it?"

"No," says Kerry. "You're still beautiful, Apple Head." The ghastly hysterectomy scar on her older sister's slim young stomach does disturb Kerry. She's afraid to have children, afraid not to have the option to have children. When Claire *went under the knife*, Kerry was consumed by anxiety. What if something happens, some mistake? She kept her fears to herself and vowed to go for a pap smear, something she had avoided since watching Jeremy Irons play twin gynecologists in *Dead Ringers*.

Piotr has the apartment to himself. *Thank God, the girls are taking a sauna.* His phone begins to ring, but he ignores it. Claire's girlfriend, Max, leaves a message on the tape. She sounds concerned, loving. He quickly rewinds over it. He will mention at some point that his machine is on the fritz; bloody girls will probably try to fix it. He notices the camera battery recharging and unplugs it. He pauses, cord in hand, and looks up at his reflection in the hallway mirror. A tight-lipped old man stares back.

Lively chatter in the hallway, a key slides into the lock. Piotr plugs the battery charger back in. He feels himself begin to crumble.

Kerry and Claire run in slow motion, both awkward in this serious moment. Uncle Piotr is hunched on the floor with his back to them. They are afraid he is having another stroke. "Uncle Piotr!" they call; they are shrill like schoolgirls. He warns them away with a sharp jerking motion of his arms, like a conductor bringing up the orchestra. They kneel on either side of him, hands fluttering. "It's okay, it's okay."

They sound like birds. "ISokee, iSokee." His arms return to his sides. He feels his nieces touching him and wonders if they are looking at each other above his bent head. "ISokee, iSokee," they repeat.

The next morning they drive past the strip malls that line the road to the Edmonton airport. No one mentions the night before: Uncle Piotr dragged himself into his den to sleep; he claimed to have a stomach cramp. Claire made him an Alka Seltzer; he accepted it without looking at her.

Kerry has graciously taken the Death Seat. A woman driving an orange Volvo waves Uncle Piotr into the crowded lane he is trying to enter. He waves back with an incredulous look on his face. "Well, that doesn't happen very often."

Kerry and Claire glance at one another. They have made a let's-be-nice pact.

"I hate to say it," says Uncle Piotr, "but it's usually a woman who won't let you into a lane."

"Alberta drivers, eh?" quips Kerry, fangs out. She looks at her watch. In two hours they'll be in Vancouver; they'll be home.

Kerry and Claire hug their uncle goodbye. The Edmonton airport isn't particularly busy. It feels small and friendly, like a bus terminal. Uncle Piotr has insisted on getting them a cart for their two small bags. After they hug, he grips the metal handle as though checking it for sturdiness. He has tears in his eyes. Kerry puts her hand over one of his and squeezes it. She feels something like longing, or heartburn, in her chest.

"Thanks for everything, Uncle P."

"Yeah, it was great." Claire sounds awkward, sad.

Uncle Piotr nods, shrugs and smiles. He lets go of the cart. Kerry puts her hands where his were; the metal is warm and damp.

Uncle Piotr drives back from the airport. He loves to drive, even if that idiot doctor told him that he shouldn't. What is it about doctors that makes him *so blame mad*? He congratulates himself again for turning down a chance to go to medical school. Someone had to look after the store. Someone had to do the dirty work. He drifts across the dotted line. A loud horn blast shocks him back into his own lane. Heart pounding—he pulls over. *Maybe I'll just rest for a while.* He reclines his seat.

It's great to have the car to myself again. Piotr admires the stunning fall day in his beautiful Edmonton. A bright blue silo with the words, "Alberta Wheat Pool" winks at him. *I'll pick up a barbecued chicken on the way home.* Piotr's mind wanders. He starts to doze; the rhythm of the passing traffic feels comforting. His hand drops to his side and brushes against something cold between the seats. He is startled awake. Piotr pulls out a tube of lipstick. *Dollie's?* He takes off the lid and runs the waxy substance on his fingertip. He sees his sister laughing on the beach: her radiant red smile. Then he remembers Kerry putting the lipstick on in the car the night he took them to the Citadel Theatre. Piotr puts the cap back on and sticks the little tube in his shirt pocket. He keeps his hand there. Through the thin polyester, he can feel the skirmish of his heart.

Giant Step

Vedder, BC, 1980

"I'll have a fur burger and a side of thighs." The boy laughs open-mouthed, showing brown teeth and a purple tongue.

Kerry figures he's been eating Pixie Stix or some other dyed candy. She keeps making popcorn. It's her job. Cheryl deals with the customers.

Cheryl Jack is the Chilliwack Drive-in snack bar manager and cashier. She's around Kerry's age, sixteen. Cheryl's nice enough, strict though. She doesn't let Kerry slack off. Cheryl stops filling the plastic stir stick container and takes the order.

"Don't got no fur burgers. Pick somethin' else." Cheryl doesn't seem afraid of Purple Tongue, even though he's one of the Bailey Boys. She never acts like she knows what these greaseballs are getting at. She says fur burger the same way she'd say cheeseburger.

"Maybe I'll have that bony little popcorn girl fer pickin' my teeth." He laughs harder this time.

Kerry imagines her body held like a toothpick being crammed into pockets of plaque, digging around in that steaming trash-heap of a mouth. She gags. The scoop of oily orange muck that she was about to feed to the popcorn machine falls face down on the floor. Cheryl looks at her, alarmed.

"Mr. Wright's gonna be here soon—*shit, girl.*"

Kerry uses a napkin to push the lump back into the scoop. She's lifting it into the garbage can when Mr. Wright staggers in. He's drunk again.

The movie plays on speakers inside the snack bar to let the girls know how close they are to having a rush of customers. This week it's *Looking for Mr. Goodbar*.

Diane Keaton is making lusty animal noises when Mr. Wright corners Kerry. "That product you're tossing away is worth more than your labour."

Kerry looks at the gob of waxy shit. Bits of hair and grit are stuck to it. Mr. Wright breathes heavily, sending her a Scotchy breeze. *What would Donna Parker do in a situation like this? Something positive. Something sucky.* Somewhere on the cover of those squeaky pre-teen books, there always lurks a shadowy man. Kerry and her best pal Barb search them out. Sometimes the man is tucked cleverly onto the spine—just an outline with a crew cut and a briefcase. They read the books out loud to each other until they feel like they're pissing their pants laughing. "Donna Parker Takes a Giant Step" is their favorite. Barb wrote "Donna Parker Drops Acid" for Kerry's sixteenth birthday—*hilarious*. Kerry hides it in her junk drawer.

"Clean that off and use it, kid." Mr. Wright lurches past her. He has a routine. It's time for his boiled dog.

Cheryl hands Kerry a plastic knife without looking at her. Kerry puts the scoop of "popcorn enhancer" on the counter and cuts off the gritty part. She wraps the wrecked bit in a napkin and carries it to the garbage. It sticks to the inside of the can, a turd in the toilet that won't go down.

"Ya want some relish there, Mr. Wright?" Cheryl lugs an economy-sized jar over to where he leans against the counter, holding his snack and waiting. Mr. Wright stares at the sad grey hotdog resting in the stale bun as Cheryl pushes down the trigger on the jug and paints a zigzag of fluorescent green across it. He smiles briefly at Cheryl and gently lifts the dog to his mouth.

Kerry wonders what made Mrs. Wright run off with the mechanic from Smithers. Mr. Wright's drinking? That's what her mom says. Maybe owning a drive-in theatre was glamorous at first. Then Mrs. Wright saw how the popcorn really gets its colour. She tired of the wieners at half time, the Styrofoam cups of bitter coffee with shots of rum, watching the same movie for days at a stretch. So, she removed her little car speaker and drove away.

Mr. Wright holds the last bite of his dog in his hand. He hesitates then pops it into his mouth. *His only comfort.* Kerry can't even think about it.

"Nice ass." Kerry's boyfriend, Tim, is at the snack bar window making smooching sounds.

Kerry feels a mixture of excitement and dread at the sound of Tim's voice. She looks over her shoulder at him but doesn't leave her popcorn station; it's almost the half-time rush.

"Hey," Kerry says, blushing.

Cheryl pours coffee into cups lined up along the counter. "Yer girlfriend's busy right now."

"No law against watching her work, eh?" Tim takes a long pull on his smoke and blows it out in Kerry's direction. "Bet you're havin' a nic fit." He moves off to the side and flashes his jacket open. A mickey of lemon gin is tucked into his shirt pocket. Kerry smiles at him, trying to make a face that says, *right on!*

Tim has dark skin, chocolate eyes and curly black hair. He's a load. Kerry's mom thinks *load* sounds gross—like "load in your pants." To Kerry and her friends, a load means gorgeous. Tim's friends call him The Mexican. The gang includes: Ornament, who never talks; Zero, who's handsome but stupid; Helmet, whose thick hair is cut in a wedge; and The Mexican. They're all eighteen but hang around the high school smoking joints. Barb goes around with Zero. The four of them meet for *liquid lunch* down by the river. When Kerry and Barb get pissed before woodwork, their friends in class won't let them touch the power tools.

"Hey-eh, Mexican!" Zero stumbles up half singing Tim's nickname. At the end of Pink Floyd's *The Wall* it sounds like that's what they're singing. "Hey-eh, Mexican!" Zero always repeats his jokes, knowing he's lucky to have thought of one at all.

Tim grabs him in a headlock. They wrestle a bit.

"Okay, guys, you better beat it." Cheryl glances back at Mr. Wright who is busy mixing a drink.

"How's about *you* beat it for me?" says Tim, making Zero fall down laughing.

Kerry's face burns. She shoots Tim an angry look. He shrugs at her and puts his hand over his heart. *Only you, baby.*

"What a horny fucking movie." Zero leans in through the window and tries to lift a couple of chocolate bars. He smiles at Cheryl.

"Gonna pay for those?" she says calmly.

Mr. Wright is standing behind Cheryl within a second. He stares the boys down. *Greasy little punks.*

Zero drops the chocolate bars and backs up. Tim smiles mock sweetly at Mr. Wright before sauntering away. Kerry's heart pounds. She turns back to her popcorn. She's only filled four little bags.

The rush begins. Drunken teens, harshly made-up women and slouch-eyed middle-aged men push against the counter. Cheryl smoothly takes their money and fetches their snacks.

"Hurry up, girl," she whispers urgently to Kerry.

Kerry stuffs the bags as quickly as possible, then slops the Golden Topping on. Some bags are only three quarters full and some are spilling over. Cheryl seems embarrassed as she hands people the botched popcorn.

After the angry rush clears and the grunting resumes on the speakers, Mr. Wright takes Kerry aside.

"I have to let you go, kid, you're too slow." Mr. Wright tries to say it nicely, but his voice is heavy with alcohol and resentment.

Kerry doesn't say anything, just walks to the sink. She stares at her hands as she washes the grease off. *I'm too slow to make popcorn.*

A car party rocks Tim's Camaro. Kerry slides in beside him in the front seat. Barb is in the back wedged between Helmet and Zero. She sings aggressively over top of the ZZ Top song.

"Shut up, bitch," Zero grabs at her breasts and roughly puts his mouth over hers. Barb stops singing and necks with Zero. Helmet leans forward and watches them like the pig that he is. Kerry cranes her head and stares him down. Helmet wags his tongue at her.

Tim mixes Kerry a plastic cup full of lemon gin and Sprite. "Don't spill any, I just fuckin' polished the seats."

"I got canned." Kerry downs her drink. Saying it out loud feels worse.

"Eeeeyewwww!" Barb shrieks the Chilliwack Yodel. She's too hammered to listen to Kerry's troubles. She acts different around Zero—dumb. Maybe even mean. She doesn't act like Barb-her-best-pal, that's for sure.

"Okay, everyone fuck off now." Tim gets out of the car and flips his seat forward. "Out, out, out."

"Shit, Mexican!"

"Go get tanked in your own truck, dipstick. My old lady's been dumped from her shit-ass job."

They're snuggled in the Camaro watching the end of the movie. Kerry is on her forth lemon gin and Sprite. Tim's right, she could get a *way* better job. Drunk fucker for a boss—who needs that? Tim's getting horny watching Diane Keaton make out with some stranger she met in a bar. He licks Kerry's neck and blows in her ear. Kerry watches the screen. The stranger is becoming violent. Kerry pulls away from Tim and switches off the speaker attached to the window.

"Can we leave?"

Tim drives with one hand on the wheel, the other on Kerry's thigh. He pulls off to the side of the bumpy dirt road and parks at the edge of the river beneath a big willow tree. Kerry knows this spot well; she's gone fishing here with her dad.

Tim changes the music to something more romantic, Supertramp, *Breakfast in America*. Usually, they dry hump through their jeans until Kerry comes. Then Tim pleads for real sex. Tonight, she slumps across the seat, like an old carrot forgotten in the fridge. Tim wraps himself around her. "Dreamer" is playing, Kerry's favourite song. *So now she puts her head in her hands, oh-no.*

Kerry closes her eyes, escapes the Camaro and Tim's demanding, pepper-scented body. She sees herself rummaging through the cedar chest and finding her mother's wedding night clothes. An ivory-coloured, floor-length nightgown and a pale blue satin housecoat. Kerry slips the housecoat on over her shorts and T-shirt and walks upstairs to make iced tea. Her mother, Dollie, is on the phone. Kerry walks into the kitchen, the train of the housecoat dragging behind her. Dollie, startled, drops the phone receiver, which swings just above the floor and smacks a cupboard door.

"Sweet Kerry blue eyes," Tim clutches her crotch. She doesn't resist. Supertramp fills her head. *Oh-o-o-oh-no! What a day, a year, a life it is.*

Kerry feels her jeans being peeled off. The panties that her mom bought her at Sweet Sixteen are next. Pink rabbits and polka dots tugged away. Kerry shivers in her purple tube top. *You-oo-oo-oo-know, well, you know you had it coming to you, now there's not a lot you can do . . .*

She can smell the Golden Topping that splashed down her front, a greasy, chemical scent. Tim unzips his fly and pushes his own jeans down. He's not wearing any underwear. Kerry glances at his penis.

"Okay . . . go ahead." Kerry closes her eyes again. Tim went down on her once after swimming. *Heaven.*

Without hesitating, Tim shoves his jacket under Kerry's bum and thrusts into her. Piercing pain.

"Ouch!" Kerry is crying. *Nothin' but a dreamer . . .*

Tim thrashes away on top of her, "*My virgin. My cherry.*"

He pulls out just before he shoots and soaks Kerry's stomach with red and white. She is shocked by the blood. So much of it. Tim rolls her panties into a wad, wipes Kerry's belly, then sticks them between her legs like a pad.

"Put your jeans back on." He licks his fingertips and wipes some flecks of blood off the upholstery.

"Can't it crawl up and make me pregnant?"

Tim laughs and ruffles her hair. "Yeah, right!"

Kerry holds the bloody wedge between her legs and hobbles out of the car. She crouches beside it and lets the blood run out onto the dirt. It forms a sticky pool. Fish guts. The sky is becoming lighter. Soon the weekend fishermen will show up. A small girl might watch as her father baits her hook and she'll hope the worm can't feel its sharp inescapable death.

THE REPLACEMENT

Kerry can't sleep. Equal parts fatigue, fury, resignation and ambition skitter across her body—warring ghost mice with blunted claws. She hasn't written so much as a journal entry in months and her new extreme social life has left her psychologically depleted. She anchors her white MacBook on top of her duvet, its comforting weight on her thighs, its blank screen waiting to be filled. She lets her hands rest on the keyboard. She types …

> *ATT: Editor, Daniel Jones*
> *Modern Love, The New York Times*
> *Submission: The Replacement, by Kerry Wiebe*

I'm spooned around a small hard object, earbuds still jammed in—another tortured night of fighting brain spam with brandy, Melatonin, and Jack Kornfield whispering meditations in my ear. My six-year-old launches herself toward me from the foot of the bed like a flying monkey. I protectively shield my iPhone—my divorce Cadillac and connection to the universe—from fifty pounds of ferocious unconditional love.

She looks at me intently and says, "If you love your iPhone so much, you should marry it."

Without time to brush my teeth, or pull a sweater over my pajama top, I find myself walking down the aisle for the second time. I'm nine years older, the sunshine, flowers, and snow-capped mountain backdrop of BC's Minter Gardens has been replaced with a dark narrow Toronto hallway. My bridesmaids, looking stunning in vintage dresses and pastel-tinted sunglasses, aren't here to pour vodka into my orange juice and make cracks about how it's *my* turn to get married and divorced. The convoy of smiling Alberta Mennonites and posse of wisecracking Vancouver cynics aren't standing by to bolster me with their large loving hits of energy: there is no father, no mother, no brothers, sisters, or ex-lovers to nudge one kitten-heeled silver slingback sandal in front of the other. There is nothing in this hallway that could compel me toward that handsome imperceptibly irritated groom who is already weary of waiting to clamp the filigreed yellow-gold band on my thin twitchy finger.

This time, instead of the passive aggressive marriage commissioner, the ceremony is officiated by my daughter who hum-sings dumb, dumb, da-dumb (as I now think of it). She pronounces us husband and wife and insists we kiss. Twice: with feeling. I find it's not that difficult to put my lips against my cold compact companion; after all, he's not promising anything he can't make good on, and he even plays Arcade Bowling with my daughter.

Satisfied, my little girl demands a wedding feast of boiled eggs and toast and suggests I "get cracking." The honeymoon is over.

A year ago, I was fretting over my dying father and exhausted mother so far away in BC. I was pounding out my TV columns, scrubbing toilets, washing dishes, roasting vegetables, and putting on fishnet body suits so my increasingly petulant mate might make like that old Marvin Gaye song and dish up some sexual healing. A year ago, I was still living with my husband—in a house so small he had to put his "junk" somewhere else. A year ago, I shut out the noise with history podcasts and Lucinda Williams, and when that didn't work, candlelit baths and confessional conversations with my matron of honor—six years buried, but still present in my waking life, my breathtaking, freckle-faced friend, "Irma of PEI."

"Want me to tell you something, Mommy? If you look down from space, you can't see the love, but it covers everything, except for a few houses."

My daughter is all about the love. She says the most beautiful, haunting things, embodies the innocence of having never been deceived. Next to her creamy goodness, I feel like a barnacle-encrusted cement block with a rusty spike protruding from it.

She has wisdom. Truly. And this iPhone marriage idea is growing on me. She's right, I am smitten with my phone, and while it may not make sweet love to me, it can do so many useful considerate things. My palm-sized sweetheart can read me to sleep, wake me gently, remind me of appointments, and help me find my way around the city. It can morph into a recorder, a flashlight, an egg timer. I can hold it up to the radio and Shazam—it tells me the name of the song *and* shows me the video.

It could be a rebound thing. After all, my iPhone was the first serious retail therapy of my new life. And, true to rebound form, it looks nothing like my husband.

Yes, my solid little friend really could be my partner in this life. Since the demise of my human marriage, my memory is not to be counted on. I do what is called "dumping." Your brain prioritizes your internal list. Unplug the iron would be at the top, for example. Eat more fruit would be at the bottom—and dumped. Occasionally I tire of playing detective. Hmm, this cup of tea is still warm— surely, I was in the bedroom recently for a reason. My steadfast iPhone can keep track of everything. I merely type all of my needs into its hard compact body, set alerts, and voila! Sheets are changed, flights are booked, forms are filled out, and birthdays are remembered. But it keeps coming back to the sex. If only . . . But that fades anyway, right?

My husband *used* to tear my clothes off on the staircase, write exquisite erotic emails, sing "Unforgettable" as we walked in the Lawrencetown tide pools, and photograph me in every possible light and position. That devolved into throwing his laundry on my desk, berating me over a missing oyster shucker, and turning my sexy sepia-toned photographs face down—likely because he wanted to write lengthy heartfelt missives to his mistress without me looking on.

Perhaps it's not so crazy to devote myself to a piece of technology. True, it doesn't have a heart, but it's also unlikely to break mine. It's a heck of a communicator, and it never makes cutting cracks about my career, intelligence, or inability to keep track of utensils. And I am getting used to bonding with inanimate objects. Strangely enough, they began communicating with me when my marriage was ending. I like to think it was really my best dead friend, Irma, possibly in cahoots with my father, sending not-so-subtle messages from that big drinking barn in the sky where it's always Happy Hour.

In the final months of our eight-year marriage, our comely Toronto cottage became like something out of *The Amityville Horror*—walls oozed rain from a leak in the roof above our bed, coat racks collapsed, and pot lights fell out of the ceiling. A printed-on-glass photograph of us in pioneer garb, taken in Nova Scotia at Sherbrooke Historical Village, hurled itself off the dresser. It smashed to the floor, slicing our image in two, beheading my cruelly handsome husband, and leaving my small white hand resting on his shoulder like a dead mouse. My Christian Dior wedding choker broke apart as I was putting on my lipstick. Rhinestones and silver beads scattering, my daughter chasing them, laughing, "Mommy needs a new necklace."

Like the blinker-eyed folks in Amityville shrugging off the shrieking from the gallows coming out of the radio, or the people in *Poltergeist* trying to make sense of their daughter disappearing into the void, I ignored the overt signs of trouble. I disregarded the dryness in my mouth, the dead look in my eyes, and those telling moments when I was all alone and in a mock jovial voice said things out loud like, "I may not be writing, but at least I'm maintaining a fiction!"

I never asked myself what my gut or these "ghosts" might be trying to tell me when they said, "Lady, listen up: your marriage was built on a graveyard—they moved the headstones, but they left the bodies in the ground!"

"Mommy, your husband is calling you!"

My black-haired beauty runs toward me holding the ringing iPhone, and it takes me a second to get the joke. Then I howl with laughter. When I don't answer it, she looks at me sternly. "You shouldn't ignore your husband, and he doesn't like that pink jacket you bought him—he's a boy."

Poor kid, she doesn't want me to blow this marriage. It pains her that I'm alone. That I can't just find someone to have another baby with like her daddy did. I try to explain that I'm not ready for a serious relationship with a new person, that I don't want another baby. I tell her that she is my love bunny, my sleeping squirrel, my euphoria. We hug like crazy people, fiercely. I can feel her strong pumping heart against my chest, her thin arms locked around me, and I think: this is enough. How lucky am I?

Is Bambi really the prince of the forest? I never think of plant-eaters as being in charge.

My daughter is not into princess culture. She finds Hannah Montana embarrassing. She loves dinosaurs,

Pokémon, and martial arts. She loves to wrestle, or as she quaintly calls it, rough house. As we rolled about on the carpet the other day, she mentioned rough housing with Daddy's girlfriend. I knew they did certain things together. They make Rice Crispy squares with Smarties in them. They walk on the boardwalk, my girl likely running ahead of the stroller barking at seagulls or chasing squirrels. For some reason I can roll with these images, the girlfriend is busy with her newborn, she's really just a nanny figure, but when the brain reel showed my blonde replacement eliciting joyful yelps from my daughter as they tousled on the rug— the fight went out of me.

I win, Mommy!

Those searchlight eyes zoom in. Does she see my sudden sadness? I want to say caustic things about Daddy's Girlfriend. I want to be a horrible hoser mom, tell her not to wrestle with that tramp—she'll get cooties. I strive for neutrality. I breathe deep yogic breaths. I think of clean sheets and vacuumed floors: stability at her father's house. I think of my daughter having a sibling. I think about the fact that my girl has at least two more people in her life to love, who love her. I think of all the positive aspects of Daddy's Girlfriend. When that doesn't work, I think of England…

Mommy, why did the chicken cross the road? He was tired of being alive.

This amazing kid is so clearly the product of two writers. And bringing her into the world is my shining moment. But still, I sometimes think it's the ultimate blonde joke that I married another writer. Writers are at once besotted with themselves and raging with insecurity. Writers have devastating remarks at the ready—and can't resist lobbing a cruel bomb. Writers tend to drink too much. Writers know how to justify drinking too much. Writers are always on deadline—especially when they want to avoid that family reunion.

Thing is, I'm a sucker for a beautiful mind. Writers tend to be deep thinkers. Writers don't say, "we partied" to describe lovemaking and then send limp text messages a day or two after said party. Writers notice details, will pay attention to your clavicle (and even know what to call it). And possibly the most sublime thing about writers in this techno age— they tend not to use emoticons. Seriously, what would Dorothy Parker do? Razors pain you ;) Rivers are damp :) Acid stains you ;) And drugs cause cramps ;) !!!

But many writers are also project orientated. They can be passionate about something for bursts and then want to move on. Start a new story. When my doctor father was dying, he wanted my mother at his side constantly. They were married for decades and rode the big wave of life deftly. They didn't expect uninterrupted ease and took myriad blows in stride. My father held my hand in the hospital and talked about my mother. His sweetheart. He couldn't stand not sleeping with her in their big bed. He didn't want to leave this life and be without his beautiful Dollie.

It hit me in that hospital room, that foul smelling, overly lit last stop, that somehow despite its promise of depth, my marriage was a thin brittle husk. My husband was not at home worrying about me and his dying father in-law—he was in a world of candlelight and perfume. Working on a new project.

A recent Facebook update of mine read, "Oh, to be shallow for even a day!" It struck a chord. It seems many of us would like to put our brains on vodka and ice. Marrying my iPhone is perhaps the ultimate shallow act, and it feels good—like a frosty beer glass against my forehead, a sweet cold sliver in my heart. I can adore it freely and know it will never trade me in for a newer model. In fact, if I manage to completely shake my inner romantic, my second husband won't even know what hit him when his thinner, sleeker upgrade pings me from across a crowded party.

> *Thank you for considering my submission. I look forward to your response.*
> *Sincerely,*
> *Kerry Wiebe*

Light snakes through the crack in her heavy curtains as Kerry stares at the screen, her finger resting on the "send" button. Her door bursts open and the flying monkey, wearing nothing but a towel tied around her neck like a cape, launches onto the bed. "I am Crazy Naked, and I will eat the Egg Men!"

Kerry pushes her computer to the side and wraps the squirming, laughing Kat in her arms. She inhales the sweetness of her daughter's slightly damp hair. Yes, this is enough.

Maybe someday "The Replacement" will just be a story: abstract, filled with outdated technology and long forgotten passion. Something for the Time Capsule: something to be discovered after the main players have moved on to new personal tragedies, unable to recall most of the details or even the broad strokes. Harmless.

Acknowledgements

Special thanks to Roslyn Muir for her constant encouragement, wisdom and everyday ass-kicking to keep me on task, and Tim Cameron for his diligent reading and assistance in getting *Toxic Shock* ready for publication. Thank you for careful reading: Mikhael Klassen-Kay, Tracy Shea Porter, and readers of my early stories: Lily Salter, Michael Shumiatcher, Gil Adamson, Ruth Ozeki, Daria Ellerman, Cindy Filipenko, Edward Kay and Mark Achbar. I'd also like to acknowledge the amazing, Genni Gunn who guided me through the first incarnation of this collection and admitted me to her generous late 90s writing group. Thank you to my lovely friend Lynn Murray, and my dear sister Kathy for inspiring me and always being in my corner.

A big thank you to the original Vancouver Slackers: Doran Aisenstat, Barrie Abbott, Christine Hare and the profoundly missed, Forbes McKay.

And finally, my wonderful friend, Donald Macomish McGregor, who passed away in 2021, for championing my writing when I needed it the most, and his beloved wife (the late) Julie Mason for publishing my first short story, *Uncle Piotr* in Canadian Forum.

About the Author

Jude Klassen is an author, TV writer and filmmaker known for her urban feature films, *Love in the Sixth*, and *Stupid For You* that combine comedy, music, family and living in the Sixth Extinction. Her short fiction has been published in the late great Canadian Forum (*Uncle Piotr*), it has been short-listed for the Writers Union of Canada competition (*The Not-So-Secret, Secret Life of Angus McFee*), and this collection was awarded a Canada Council literary grant. *Western Alienation* was shortlisted for both the Toronto Life Summer Fiction issue (the final one), and This Magazine's Great Canadian Literary Hunt. *Food-Combining* was published in The Vancouver Courier. Jude was raised in the wilds of British Columbia, Canada and now lives with her son in Toronto, Ontario.

judeklassenfilmmaker.com
Instagram: @jude.klassen
X: @judecast